THE MOTHER'S THREAT

A COMPELLING DOMESTIC THRILLER

SUSAN SPECHT ORAM

THE MOTHER'S THREAT

A compelling domestic thriller

SUSAN SPECHT ORAM

SOS Communications LLC

Published by SOS Communications LLC in 2023

www.susanspechtoram.com

First Edition

Cover design by Best Page Forward

ISBN: 979-8-9870410-7-9 (paperback)

ISBN: 979-8-9870410-6-2 (e-book)

❀ Created with Vellum

A NEW CLIENT

I follow my friend Wendy out of Gigi's Café and close the door with a shudder. There's a secret hidden inside the tall, old house where the café is located. I'd rather not know about it, but I can't unsee what I learned when I was young.

Wendy and I met when I was new to town, and our orders at the café for take-out coffee and scones were mixed up.

Tugging on a strand of curly hair, she says, "Let's go sailing soon."

A nervous flutter in my belly reminds me of my appointment with a bigwig in town. "I'd like to, but I'll be busy for a while. I'm signing my first client today." I flash her a weak smile. "I need to make sure everything's running smoothly before I take time off."

She fixes her green eyes on me, gazing with concern.

"Don't forget your friends and your family while you're setting up your empire. And remember, there are no woes that time on the water and the smell of salt air won't cure."

We stop at her car, and she unlocks it. "Aren't you nervous about starting your own company? What if you can't make the payroll?"

I shove my hands in my pockets and stare at a crack in the sidewalk. I've had sleepless nights worrying about money. What if Outrigger Services goes belly up?

With a shrug, I say, "The thought does keep me up at night. But I've always wanted to be my own boss, so it's worth the risk."

My mind drifts to when I was young and left on the doorstep of my dad's house. My biological mom waved and said, "Be good and prove to everyone you can take care of yourself." She took off in a cloud of exhaust, leaving me coughing before I knocked on the door.

Wendy pats me on the shoulder. "Hope your new client works out."

"Me too."

We part ways, and my muscles tense. I want to get back to the office and check on my staff. Adrenaline courses through my veins as I stride along, humming to myself.

A Porsche sports car drives past, and I nod. If things go well in the coming years, I could get one of those.

An older woman pushes two toddlers in a baby

stroller. She reminds me of my Aunt Mary and Uncle Fred. When life settles down, I've got to give them a call.

She stops at a crosswalk. Cars stop and wait. She takes her time crossing the street, but no one honks. People are fairly laid back in our corner of the country. We're out of the way, and you've got to want to be here if you came all this way.

I cover the five blocks to the office in no time. The office I rented three weeks ago is on the second floor of a brick building a block off the main drag in downtown Millersville.

The word downtown sounds big and fancy, but the truth is, I'm in a small waterfront town in the Pacific Northwest. You need a boat to drive west or north, because there's only islands around us. To say Millersville is isolated is an understatement, because it's on an island reachable by bridge from the mainland.

My pulse quickens as I run up the stairs. I've got energy to burn because today is the day we start working for our first client. Coming in the door, I pant and catch my breath.

Wiping my brow, I stand in the bullpen and nod to my crew. "Hey, guys."

We know each other well because I hired them to work at our past employer, when I was their boss and head of security. We protected a biotechnology company and its underground manufacturing facility until it became glaringly apparent that we needed to switch sides and help take the company down. When we were about to be out of work at our last company, I told them I'd start my own firm and hire them.

My three employees look up from their laptops and smile. There's a palpable feeling in the room of something important taking place.

I say, "I'm going to Bettermed to meet with Mr. Brinker. While I'm out, drill down on the plan we came up with for how to protect his company. We'll install surveillance cameras, check the feeds, monitor social media and keep an eye on his property. And do some research to generate other ideas. I want us to be fast on our feet when we have a signed contract."

In the back of my mind as I say this, I'm thinking about how we need more clients to pay rent on the office and for them to feed their families. I'm single by choice at the moment, and so is Flora. But Vincent has a newborn baby and a wife who went through an ordeal when she was pregnant and on bed rest.

My second-in-command, Mimi, is a few years younger than me, in her mid- twenties, and she just started saving for retirement. She pulls her long brown hair into a high ponytail and stands. "We're on it."

Vincent, a big, broad-shouldered man around my age, is in his early thirties. He says, "We've also fine-tuning a list of potential clients. We'll have it ready by the time you come back from your meeting." His biceps bulge, poking out of his t-shirt.

Flora, my third team member, grins. "Go get 'em, boss. Mr. Brinker will learn that Outrigger Services is the best." She tugs on the neck of the black turtleneck she always wears.

I walk to the Bettermed building, which is three blocks away on Commercial Avenue. Outside the post office, a man in an orange knit cap perches on a bench. He's playing a guitar and singing with his guitar case open on the ground. I pull five bucks out of my pocket and add it to the coins and dollar bills as he launches into a ballad.

I smile to myself and hope the times are changing, like the song. By the end of the day, my business checking account will be flush with a first payment. I grip the cold metal door handle and open the door to my client's lobby.

Striding in, I check in at the reception desk. Bettermed is an industry leader in creating inventory control software for hospitals, pharmacies, and long-term care facilities. The company could be located in Seattle or another big city, but the founder and president picked Millersville because he lives here. A lot of wealthy, powerful people live in our area or have second homes in the San Juan Islands. They're hiding in plain sight, but if you stop at the specialty wine shop, you'll get a look at them during the wine tastings there.

Two employees walk past me looking at their phones on the way out the door. Bettermed's coding geeks are well paid and tend to wear tight pants, yellow high-end running shoes and blue or white or tortoise shell framed glasses.

I say to the receptionist, "Hello, I'm Violet Cleveland. I'm here to see Bob Brinker."

The gal behind the counter looks about twenty years old, maybe fresh out of community college. She checks my identification, and a diamond in her nose sparkles. Thin blond hair hangs limp below her shoulders.

I run a hand through my short hair while I assess the company's approach to security. If it's lax, we'll hire security guards to augment the receptionist's services. A guard standing behind the desk with her would communicate they were serious about security, and that this is not a company to mess with.

Although she glances at my identification, she doesn't note it in a log. I sign in with my name, the date and time, and she points to the elevator.

"Take the elevator to the fourth floor. His assistant will greet you there."

Going to the elevator, I made a note to suggest to my client that he change the registration process and have visitors write down their driver's license or passport numbers. If anyone coming in violates security measures, we'll know exactly who they are and be able to provide that to the police.

The elevator glides up to the top floor, and my stomach knots. This is it, the new beginning I've always wanted. When the elevator doors slide open. I step out, armed with my lucky pen from the Brown Lantern, my favorite bar, and head toward my brilliant future. Or so I hope.

His assistant stands and ushers me into a large office facing the waterfront. Down below, I catch a glimpse of the port shed building next to Cedar Channel, where I've sailed on Wendy's boat. The water is a deep blue today with few waves.

I sigh. I just have to get him to sign the contract and get out of here. It'll be a routine assignment for us and almost boring for my team. We've handled turmoil in the past, but in a small town, people don't come to cause trouble. They come to relax and lower their blood pressure.

Mr. Brinker is the president and founder of Bettermed. My team's research shows he's often quoted in the news as an industry expert. He's also the current president of the Software Trade Alliance with a two-year term. The trade association's members include all the movers and shakers in the software industry.

He stands at his desk and comes over, shaking my hand. He's in his fifties, and his silver hair is cut just so, like a movie star's hair.

A flicker of worry flits across his face, making me wonder what's bothering him. If it's about his security concerns, I'll find out after we sign the contract and the non-disclosure agreement. It's my goal not to be caught unawares. My business is to protect the client, and that's impossible if I don't know about the risks they face.

When Brinker and I sign the documents, my hand is slick with sweat. My pulse picks up. I stack the papers and smile, acting like I sign on new clients every day.

Before I leave his office, I say, "I'll set up a regular meeting. We'll go over security concerns and review what our monitoring picks up."

"Excellent." He holds up an index finger. "And there's one more thing you should know. Next week, Bettermed is hosting a trade association meeting here in our offices. It'll be members of the Software Trade Alliance or STA steering committee, and we'll meet in the conference room downstairs. The last thing I want is a bunch of protesters marching around the building, making a scene while we're holding discussions. You and your team need to shut down any malcontents and nutjobs."

I swallow hard and flex my jaw. He didn't mention the upcoming meeting until now. Yesterday, I said to my team, "This'll be easy money. How much trouble can a software company get into?" We all laughed.

I say, "Why are you holding the meetings here and not in Seattle or another city?"

He taps a thick finger on his desk. "I suggested it."

I cock my head. "Shouldn't an event like that be held in a city and not in a small town?"

He nods. "You may be right, but I wanted to keep it close to home so we'd control the narrative. And I wanted to show off our area and where I live. I'm bringing you onboard to get ahead of the situation before the meeting."

I cross my arms. A week doesn't give my team much time to prepare and prevent disaster. "What else do I need to know?"

He runs a hand through his silver movie-star perfect hair. "Reporters have been calling. They've heard rumors about possible protests."

I sink into a seat. I'd thought I was here for a quick in-and-out contract signing, but there's much more afoot and happening at a faster pace than he let on when we first met.

"I didn't hear you mention protests before. Let's go over the situation now in detail. I need to be prepared so we can protect you."

His face is pale. From the dark circles under his eyes, it looks like he hasn't been getting much sleep. If this is worrying him that much, I might be working long nights and staying up late in the days ahead.

Running his hands down his drawn face, he says, "My sources at the trade alliance tell me people are planning to come here from all over the country to protest next week. Various organizations will join forces. They want to make a statement in Millersville."

I nod. "Tell me about the groups. Who might be involved?"

He ticks off a list on his fingers. "We've got animal rights activists defending turtles and dolphins, people opposing server farms, groups protecting the environment and those who are adamant against companies listening to conversations on their devices."

I rub my chin. "We've got a grab bag of causes, and some of them are not without merit. This will be interesting. Is there a valid reason why your company would be targeted?"

"No, I don't think so."

"So, we could have a bunch of people headed to town who may be looking for a visible place to make a statement and get media attention. And you and your company just happen to be in the line of fire?"

"Yes, that's what I think. I've even received a letter with a vague threat."

He opens a drawer and pulls out a white piece of paper. His hands shake.

I jump up. "Don't touch that. We might be able to get fingerprints off it."

He sets the paper down. "Good point."

I snap on a pair of disposable non-latex gloves and lift the page off his desk.

I read the typed words aloud. "Your industry pollutes the environment. Server farms harm the planet. People's privacy is at stake. Stop spying on us with computers. If you don't stop the STA meeting, you'll regret it."

I arch my eyebrows, wondering who wrote the letter and what they have planned. "Someone is ticked off. And you're right, this is a vague threat, but we'll take it seriously."

He sighs. "There have been quiet rumblings directed at the STA, but we've managed to keep it out of the public eye so far. I was hoping to avoid an ugly situation by holding the steering committee meetings here. I convinced them by saying we'd keep a low profile in a small town."

My neck tenses. I resist the urge to loosen it like I always do, looking left and right and up and down. "Unfortunately, that's not possible these days. Activists devour crumbs of information and follow a trail. They can blow up a corporate event and make it into a dangerous situation."

I pull a plastic document holder from my briefcase and slide the letter inside. "Did this come in an envelope and do you still have it?"

He shrugs. "My assistant who works on Saturdays threw it out."

"What's their name?"

"Lydia, Lydia Barker. She's finishing high school and helping me out. She wants to work for me after high school and move up the ranks." He chuckles. "She's got more ambition than either of my kids, who're older. What a shame."

I nod, reminded of how my step-mom was disappointed when I joined the Army. She's more of a peacenik and wanted me to work for a non-profit and save the world. "You never know, your kids' ambitions might strike later. Children need to find their way, and it's not always how parents envision things."

He glances at a photo on the credenza of a grinning young woman and young man with their arms draped around each other's shoulders. "Those are my mischievous two. My wife insisted on calling them Boots and Guns. But she's gone now." He wipes his eyes.

Clearing my throat, I say, "I'm sorry the hear that. My condolences."

He waves a hand in the air. "Oh, my wife didn't die. She just up and left us. But that's a story for another day. Right now, we have bigger concerns. Like the trade meetings that are starting on Monday."

I grit my teeth. My company just signed on as Brinker's security consultant, and we're already in a hot mess.

I glance outside and consider what we're up against. We've got a whole lot of unknowns to tackle back at the office. The sky is blue, and it's a beautiful day. But with a shudder, I sense a storm is brewing and on the way.

After I question him and gather more details, I head back to brief my team. Walking along Commercial, a soft breeze ruffles my hair. My body buzzes with energy.

My hunch was right. I won't be going sailing any time soon. We've got a load of work to do to get ready for the trade association talks.

1

On the way to the office, I call my mom to check in. She lives on a farm with twenty other people near Olympia, our state capital to the south. I call it a commune, but she bristles at that label, saying the group is about living in tune with the earth, not free love. It's not a lifestyle I'd pick, and it's too unstructured for me, but she gravitated to the group after Dad divorced her and took up with a much younger woman.

When she picks up, I say, "Hey, just checking in to see how you are." I can't resist making a wise crack, so I add, "How's life at the commune?"

"Violet, you know we're not like that. It's an intentional community of like-minded people who are devoted to protecting the earth and stopping big corporations from taking over our lives."

I roll my eyes. "How are the eggplants growing? Have you got many tomatoes?"

"Well, now that you mention it, we do have a bumper crop of tomatoes. The trouble is, we're leaving in a few days to head north, and we'll be out of town for a week or so. A neighbor will come by and take care of the chickens and harvest the produce while we're away, but I'm worried some of the food will spoil. Can you come down and manage things? You're so responsible. You're the perfect person to fill in while I'm away."

I shake my head. "I can't. Remember, I started my own company? I signed my first client today." A swell of pride fills me, and I look up at a white puffy cloud in a blue sky.

She croons. "That's wonderful, dear. You know how to get things done. I've always admired that about you."

"Have you heard from Dad?"

"Nope, and that's fine with me. How about you?"

I wince. "No, but I was hoping he'd remember my birthday."

My dad and I were close when I was young, and I followed him into the military. Daisy, the woman who raised me, didn't want me to be in danger, so I never let her know what hazards I faced during my time in the Army.

A thought occurs to me, so I say, "You said you were headed north. Where are you going?"

She hesitates before answering. "I'll fill you in later when the details are settled."

She sounds secretive, which is unlike her. "Stay safe, and let me know where you are. Love you."

When I hang up, I let out a low whistle. My mom isn't the prim and proper mother with a perfect short bob cut who I grew up with. She let her hair grow long and wears caftans when she isn't working in the fields. She laughs a lot and calls herself Daisy now. Who knows where she and her group are headed? Probably some retreat center with meditation and meatless Monday kind of place, where they'll talk about organic soil, heirloom tomatoes, and ancient grain seeds.

I open the office door and rush inside. My pulse quickens. "Gather round, we've got a challenge ahead of us. For the next two weeks, it'll be all work and little sleep. Tell your families you're on assignment and not to expect you home much, if at all."

Mimi groans. "What's the urgency about? After Chaos Corporation crashed, we wanted work. But I didn't expect to dive into 24/7 work so fast."

"Shine your boots, and get your game faces on," I say, looking around the group. My team members are hand-picked for readiness in response. My eyes land on each one, assessing their attitude. "Are you ready to dive in and nail this assignment?"

"Yes," they say, thumping the table with fists.

I grin. The energy level is high. We are armed for battle.

I say, "The protesters won't expect a small town like

Millersville to have a skilled security team waiting in the wings. We're their worst nightmare, and they won't see us coming."

We pump fists in the air, and I drag a chair over and take a seat.

"Okay, boss," Vincent says. "Give us the rundown."

"The situation is mission critical and messed up at the outset, I'll admit. Brinker just told me a trade association meeting will take place in town on Monday. Rabble rousers are talking about coming here and protesting."

Flora, who is younger than the rest of us, says, "Why here? There aren't enough places to stay in Millersville, are there?"

I say to her, "Call around and see if the motels and hotels are booked for next week. I bet they are. And check on that RV campground too. If I'm right, the protesters will bunk down there in tents."

"Got it."

To Vincent, I say, "We need to draft statements to provide to Brinker and his team in case the situation erupts. Draw up a list of measures to take and get me a rundown of how long each step in the process will take. Who will guard entrances to Bettermed? Do we need to barricade off the building? Where are we sourcing materials from to prevent people from attacking trade delegates or harming the property?"

Mimi says, "I'll get in touch with the police and be the liaison." She glances at me and adds, "But you know the police chief, so let me know if you talk to him. Do you think anyone's talked with the police about the possible protests?"

"I don't think so," I say. "But Brinker said reporters have been calling him for a statement about the organized protest. His trade association expects a coalition of protesters from various organizations around the U.S."

I rattle off the list of splinter groups Brinker gave me and point to Mimi. "Put your ear to the ground and give me a list of potential groups who're likely to show up. Who's posting online about this? Which groups are planning on showing up in town? What's the tone of the online chatter?"

I drum my fingers on the armrest of the chair and say, "We only a week to prepare, but I know we can do it. We'll protect Brinker and his staff and the building. You are the best. I hand-picked you to work for me, and now we've accepted a new challenge. We'll prove ourselves with this client, and after that, others will want to sign on."

They nod, and their eyes shine. Their jaws tense.

I say, "I want to know who is behind the various protest groups and their backgrounds. How are they communicating? Which social media channels are they using to post messages and rile people up? Mimi, will you handle that?"

"I'm on it."

I say, "I'll call the police chief and mayor since I know them and report back. Any questions?"

Flora raises her hand. "Why isn't the company's in-house security team handling this? What did they say when you met with them?"

I blow out a breath. She has a tendency to go on the negative and can sound like she's whining without realizing it. I've got to shut it down before her attitude infects the others.

I shrug. "Believe it or not, they don't have one. They didn't see a need for in-house security team yet. But Brinker received a threat. Who wants to handle interviewing the assistant who opened the mail?"

Mimi raises her hand. I can always rely on her to step up and shoulder responsibilities, and for that, I'm grateful.

I stand and say, "It's possible it may amount to nothing. But we need to be prepared, even if no one shows up. Are you up for this assignment?"

"Yes," my staff says.

"Will you be ready?"

"Hell, yeah," they say, standing and grinning.

"Great, then let's show our first client what we can do."

I walk into my office and close the door. After being employed by a large company before, I have a new weight on my shoulders with running my own firm. I cross my fingers and hope we'll prove ourselves next week. If not, my new company will go bust, and I'll be out of business.

2

———————

Closing my office door, I call the chief of police, Cliff Stafford. His assistant puts me through to him right away. We've known each other since I came to town, which was four years ago.

"Chief, how are you? This is Violet. Have you heard about the potential situation next week in town? People might show up to protest the software trade association meeting."

He clears his throat. "I've been briefed about it, yes. From what we hear, it's a bunch of loud mouths spouting off. We don't think anyone will show up."

I tilt my head. "I'm not sure about that. My team is working on ferreting out how credible the threat is so we can be prepared. Did Brinker mention the threat he received to you?"

"He did, when I saw him at the Rotary banquet the

other night. He didn't sound concerned, so we weren't going to look into it unless he wanted to pursue it. He didn't sound concerned."

"I have the letter with the threat. Can you run it through the fingerprint system? I'd hate for us to be wrong and drop it if these people are serious. We don't want to look like fools later."

He chuckles. "No, we don't. Send it over, and we'll run it through the system. We've never had trouble in this town with protesters, and I don't expect that to change. What harm can a bunch of do-gooders do over a few days?"

I raise my eyebrows. In my experience, a hell of a lot can happen in a short time. Like the fiasco Martin Truex, the now-jailed head of Chaos Biotech created. But that's in the past, and I have a new start now.

"Thanks very much," I say. "I'll send someone over with the item in question. Next on my list is to call the mayor."

"Good luck with that. She's up to her ears with the public comments on the new zoning plan. Everyone's an expert these days. Not in my backyard is what they're saying about high-density housing."

"We need it. My people need to live in town to be ready for emergencies and call outs, but it's tough for them to find housing they can afford."

"You know what the answer is?" he says. "Pay them

more. From what I heard from Bob Brinker, he's paying you enough to spread it around."

I arch an eyebrow. No one has secrets in this small town. "When I get a few more clients, I just might do that. Right now, my team needs to prove we can handle any chaos around the trade association talks next week."

The chief laughs. "I think you're taking this way too seriously. It's all rumors. If I were you, I'd leave the office early and head over to Anthony's for a martini. I'll be there later today if you want to stop by."

I smile. Anthony's is a bit high-brow style for me, with the movers and shakers. I'm more comfortable at the Brown Lantern. Patrons don't have a water view there and can't see any boats afloat, but the sports pennants on the walls and baseball and basketball games on TV make me feel at home. I was the best softball pitcher in my high school, and my shoulder still complains about it and tells the story.

"I might see you there, but probably not until after next week. I want to buckle down and get my arms around the potential situation before trouble breaks out."

"All right then. We'll be in touch if we find a match for any fingerprints on the document."

We hang up, and I go into the kitchen area to grab a Coke. My throat is parched from talking so much in the last few hours. I open the frig door, and cold air cools my face.

I fan my armpits. I'm perspiring from getting riled up

about a pending crisis, and I want to prove myself as the owner of a new business. But you won't be getting me to sign up for the Chamber of Commerce. I plan to be way too busy the first few years to do that. Maybe later down the road, I'll network with other businesspeople.

"Boss," says Vincent, his eyes wide. "I got something. Come check this out."

I grab a can of pop and follow him to his work station.

He sits at his computer and points to the screen.

"Read that. It's written by that reporter at *The Stranger*, the one who covered the story about Chaos Biotech."

Reading aloud, I say, "A storm is brewing two hours north of Seattle in the town of Millersville. Hot on the heels of breaking recent news about a biotechnology company putting profit over patient safety and compliance with regulations for clinical trial enrollment practices, sources say people are gathering from across the country to join in Millersville, two hours north of Seattle, to protest technology companies controlling personal choices by setting standards that allegedly hurt the average computer user and benefit large corporations with vested interests."

I pop the can open. Air hisses out. I scan the article and wonder how many people are headed our way.

I take a sip of cold Coke and say, "Thanks for showing this to me. Good work. It looks like we have a real situation on our hands, doesn't it?"

He nods. "I'll keep you informed as I learn more about the groups behind this."

Squinting at his computer screen, I say, "Ned named some groups: Pelicans United, Tortoises for Freedom, The Healthier Lives Coalition."

I tap my chin, mulling over a stray unwanted thought. Could my mother be involved in the fomenting trouble? I don't think she'd show up where I live without telling me first. But it is possible she'd join with naysayers who are rallying against big business. That's her passion. Participating in organized protests brings a smile to her face.

"Get your ears to the ground, everyone," I say to my team, who are hunched over laptops. "We'll treat it as a real threat to Brinker's business from now on. Find out everything you can about the organizers and where they're staying. Get a mole inside the group. I want inside information stat."

I call the mayor before I head out for the day. It helps that I know her assistant from when I worked in town heading up Chaos Biotech's security team. I tell her a joke and then she patches me through to Gloria Rothman.

"Honorable Mayor," I say, "May I have a moment of your time?"

She scoffs. "Come off it, Violet. Of course, I have time for you. What's up?"

"Are you at all concerned about the trade association meeting being held in town next week? I'm hearing that protesters will flood into Millersville, join forces, and make life difficult for those who live here. They want to make a united stand, and they picked our town to do it."

"You're a worrier, and that's what I like about you. When I need a down to earth slant on an issue, I come to you. So no, I'm not concerned. But tell me what you think. I'm interested in your perspective."

"First of all, have you read the latest article in *The Stranger*? About people planning to show up here and rock the boat?"

"No, I haven't." She chuckles. "I don't believe what the papers say, anyway. They're always looking for an angle and stirring up conflict."

I shake my head. "In this case, what you see in the news may be correct. My sense is it's not rumors, it's fact. I think you and the police chief need to be prepared to be deluged next week with people carrying protest signs."

"This is the first I've heard of anyone taking this seriously. I'll make you a bet. I say this'll blow over like a leaf in the wind and be gone before you know it. If I'm right, you owe me a beer at the Brown. Listen, I've got to go. Keep me abreast of what you learn. I want to be informed."

"I'll do that," I say. "And let's hope I'm wrong."

Hanging up, I have a sinking feeling my team is in for a series of long nights.

3

The next morning, I call the trade association and ask for the name Brinker gave me.

"Hold, please," a woman says.

Elevator music plays, repeating the same canned tune every thirty seconds. I grit my teeth. No wonder people fly into rages over the phone at customer service specialists.

Four minutes later, and I know because I'm timing my wait, a woman comes on the line. "Marleen Hooper, Communications. How can I help you?"

"Hi, I'm Violet Cleveland, and my firm has been hired to handle security issues for Bettermed and Mr. Brinker. I'd like to be sure we're working together and share our plans for the potential protests next week."

She laughs. "That's all talk. There's no substance to the rumors. We give no credence to the idea that anyone will show up in your little town with picket or protest signs.

We discussed it at our senior roundtable, and the decision was unanimous to ignore it. We have a crisis plan ready, if we need to fall back on that. But I can guarantee it won't happen. It'll just be a bunch of boring tech execs meeting around a conference table. No one cares about that. Don't you agree?"

She slurps a beverage. I'd pick her, from her dismissive attitude just now, as a skinny latte gal. She's probably looking out from her office over the Hudson River and can't wait to get off the phone with me, a West Coast bumpkin.

She doesn't realize it, but I'm an expert in ferreting out information using sophisticated software. No one can beat me at intelligence gathering. That's why heads of companies hire me.

I clear my throat and say, "Down on the ground where the action is likely to take place, we have a different attitude. We're taking the rumors seriously. My staff is looking into crowd control measures."

She snorts. "What's next? Paddy wagons?"

I bite my lip. "We are prepared, if needed, to haul offenders away on buses."

"Oh, come on. A whiff of what might happen has shaken you locals to your toes? Get realistic. Millerstown isn't the center of the universe, you know."

My jaw clenches. This woman is downright rude with her city-slicker know-it-all view. "The name of our town is Millersville. And my staff and I at Outrigger Services will be prepared, even if you and your team choose to be blindsided."

"Let's keep in touch. You'll let me know if the threats are real, won't you? I have another issue that's a priority and calling for my attention, an urgent matter."

"Whatever," I say. "Here's my cell. Call me when you come to town, and we can meet."

"Oh, I'm not going to the meeting in person. I'm sending a communications specialist. She'll handle any concerns that arise. I can assure you this is a non-issue."

"What is her cell number then? And I'd like to have yours too, in case things get out of hand."

"No need for that," she says. "Belinda will arrive the night before. I'll tell her to contact you."

I hang up and frown, flopping back in my office chair. We might as well be marooned on Cedar Island, across the channel. We're the only ones preparing for a crisis.

Going out to the bullpen, I get their attention by saying, "Heads up, everyone. We're alone in this. The mayor, the police chief and the trade association aren't concerned about people coming to protest. They're brushing it off as rumors."

Vincent crosses his arms. Mimi furrows her eyebrows. Flora lets out a low whistle.

I say, "We can't rely on anyone else. If a storm hits, I'll reach out to the trade association contact, the police, and the mayor. But I want you to know this may not go down easy. Tell your families you're going to be busy and not to expect to see you until the trade meeting is over. We rescued people at the secret detention center on Cedar Island, and now we're tackling a project that's just as difficult. I want us to be prepared to control a crowd of passionate activists seeking attention for their causes. Let's get ready."

"Right, boss." They nod and go back to work.

A phone rings. It's the landline I set up in case of an earthquake when the cell towers are flooded with calls and overloaded.

I pick up the phone and answer it. "Outrigger Services, how can I help you?"

A woman whispers, "Don't tell anyone where you heard this. But there's going to be a planning meeting for protesters at the Depot downtown tomorrow. Protest leaders are coming into Millersville in the morning. They'll pretend they're tourists, but they're out to change the world. Can you get someone down to the Depot to monitor what they say? The meeting will start at two p.m. If you send someone, make sure they don't say where they work. Be anonymous. Blend in."

I'm writing furiously on a pad of paper, taking notes and hoping I've got the details down correctly. "Who is this?"

She muffles the phone. "I can't say."

I repeat what she told me. "Do I have that right?"

"Yes," she says in a quiet voice. "I've got to go."

With a click, she hangs up.

Who was she? Is this a real lead or a false trail?

I go over to Mimi and tell her what I just heard. "I think we need to treat this as reliable information, just in case. Do you agree?"

She nods. "Definitely. Someone needs to go to that meeting. But I can't. I've got too much to do around here."

Glancing around the room, my staff have their heads down and are focused on their separate tasks. I need them to keep working. If we're going to succeed, we need to protect our client, prove ourselves, and get word out about us being the go-to security services firm.

I say, "I'll handle this. I'll stay out of sight, listen in, and report back."

4

———

The next afternoon, I'm wearing jeans, a t-shirt, and black boots. I pull on a wig with blue green hair and wave to the team. "Wish me luck. I'm heading out to the meeting."

"Be discreet," Mimi says. "Keep your head down and study the floor. Don't make eye contact or give out your name. Make one up if you have to."

I pat her on the back. "You don't need to school me in undercover work. Remember, I got years on you in this business."

She smiles. "Just thought a reminder might not hurt. I wonder if you'll see anyone you'll recognize when you're there?"

I shake my head. "No way I'll know anyone at the meeting. It'll be a bunch of wing nuts talking about making protest signs or turtle costumes." A thought crosses my mind. "But there is one small possibility, now that I think about it."

"Oh?" she says, studying my face.

"My mother did say she was heading up north on a trip, but she wouldn't say where she was going." I cock my head. "Would she come here and not mention it to me? I doubt it. Her group of friends wouldn't disrupt a trade association summit. They don't care about things like that."

My brows furrow, because after my dad divorced her, and for that I haven't forgiven him, our roles reversed. She moved to the farm and is living off the land. She insists I call her Daisy. I became the responsible adult, managing a team of experts and starting my own company.

I slip into the Depot a few minutes after the meeting starts so no one will introduce themselves to me or ask who I am. Sitting on the floor near the exit door, I hunch over and keep my eyes down, listening for actionable intelligence.

I glance around the room and don't see any familiar faces. Thank goodness my mother isn't here. That would pose too much of a conflict for me, if she was on the opposite side on the protest lines. Would I have the courage to tell a police officer to haul her off to jail if needed? Or spray her with pepper spray? I don't think so, and I don't even want to think about it.

A tall man in his early thirties with a long brown beard stands and talks about protesting at nearby companies. A guy who looks like a college student in his late teens suggests the group go to Weyerhaeuser, a major timber company, and picket, because of its clear-cutting practices.

"It doesn't make sense to go there," the tall man says. "That company is maybe three hours south of here. We want to protest companies in town for harming the environment and spying on us. Does anyone know companies in this area to target?"

My jaw drops when I spot my mother. She has a bright-colored butterfly painted on her left cheek. She stands and raises her hand to speak. I whip my head down and stare at the Depot's worn floor boards.

My stomach knots. What is she doing here? What will she say? I hope she won't mention me. Please, Daisy, don't say anything about me.

But as if my thoughts had attracted the exact opposite of what I want, my mother says, "My daughter, Violet Cleveland, owns a security services company here, and her client is a software company headquartered in Millersville."

"What's the name of her company, and the one she works for? Where does she live?" a guy in a black sweatshirt says.

"She used to work for Chaos Biotechnology and then, as you likely read in the news, they folded, and the head of that company was arrested for holding hostages on Cedar Island. After that, she started a consulting firm called Outrigger Services. Her client is where they'll be holding the trade association meetings."

My stomach plummets. Hairs on my arms stand on end. Doesn't she have any common sense? My mother is divulging my personal details and jeopardizing my safety. I'm her daughter. Doesn't she care?

I hang my head and close my eyes. Please stop. Don't go any further. I love you, why are you doing this? For ego strokes? To position yourself as a leader? You don't need to do this to prove yourself to the group. Don't expose me, Mom, protect me. Don't make my life harder just when I'm starting over with a new business, and the team is depending on me for paychecks.

"She's protecting Bettermed, and she lives at 133 Oak Drive."

My eyes flash open. My brows furrow. My forehead wrinkles.

How could my mother have put me in harm's way?

Is she so enmeshed in her cause that family ties don't matter?

What if one of these well-meaning, fervent zealots turns up at my house and breaks in and hurts me? How could she do this?

I clench my jaw and cross my arms, poking a finger at my Smith & Wesson .38 Special five shot snub nose revolver in my underarm gun holster. The snooze fest is over. This just became real. It's about to get ugly in town and within my own family.

"Thanks, Daisy," the tall leader says. "You've provided excellent information we can use. Everyone, I want you to make a list of local targets, like Daisy's daughter's company, her client, her home, and other locations in town. We want the most visibility and press coverage when we protest."

A woman with purple hair and a lined face says, "If we post drum circles outside those locations, it'll distract them from their work. We'll need megaphones."

The Leader nods. "Great call, Zamby. I like how you're thinking. We'll create noise and drive them crazy so they can't get anything done. We're expecting five hundred people, and maybe more will come. They'll camp in the bushes, pitch tents on sidewalks, whatever it takes to be on hand to join our parades. We've applied for permits for marching down Commercial, so we're set for that. We need someone to organize food lines. Any volunteers?"

"I'll handle it," a clean-shaven man says, brushing blond hair out of his eyes.

A college-age student stands and plays with the zipper on her blue hoodie. She says, "Too bad Chaos Biotechnology went out of business. They would've been a perfect target to protest and get loads of media attention."

"You're right," the Leader says. "But we'll get TV and newspaper coverage with the activities we have planned. I don't want to say too much now, in case there are spies in the room. But it's gonna be a blow out. And you'll all be glad you were here for the biggest protest of the decade." He raises his right fist.

People stamp their feet. Applause erupts. A guy near me cups his hands and hoots.

The leader says, "That's right, this will be the biggest protest of the decade."

The crowd of thirty or forty people claps and cheers.

A shiver runs through me. They're expecting a lot of people, and the police aren't prepared. I tie the laces on my boots and turn up the corners of my mouth, doing my best to look pleased.

When the discussion turns to making turtle and dolphin costumes, I slip out the door before the meeting breaks up. I don't want to be asked who I am or what I'm doing here.

These people are smarter than I'd expected. They know what they're doing, and we'd better take them seriously. If the mayor and police chief refuse to do that after I brief them, my staff and I will. Someone needs to step up, and it might as well be me and my team. We're wired from birth to spring into action and protect others. We're your unsung heroes, and that's fine with us.

I frown, recalling how my mother gave out my address and exposed me. I need to protect myself and be more vigilant about keeping an eye out when I'm off duty. Striding back to the office, my pulse races with the news of the biggest protest of the decade coming to town.

To be closer to the action and defend my company, I'll

move into the office and sleep on a cot. It'll be easier than trying to navigate traffic with so many visitors in town. I just hope they won't do anything to my house.

I step on a stone and stumble. Thanks a lot, Mom. After all this is over, I'm going to have a heart-to-heart conversation with her about prioritizing loved ones over causes. Family comes first, doesn't it? I always thought so until now.

5

———

When I get back to the office, I brief my staff. Flora grins and holds up her hands. "This is huge."

Vincent paces the room. "You're sure they said that? The protest of the decade?"

"Yep."

Mimi goes to the white board on the wall. "Let's get started and ramp up our plan."

"Right," I say. "We need security guards at Bettermed covering the exits."

Mimi writes that down with a blue erasable marker.

"We need to brief the employees and warn them," Vincent says.

Flora says, "We need to scout the streets and offer real-time reports on numbers of people gathering and their activities."

Mimi jots that down and adds, "Especially at our client's building."

"And in a two-block radius," Vincent says.

Mimi draws a map of downtown with a big "x" for Bettermed. We're a well-oiled machine, working smoothly as we strategize and draw up a plan. I look around the room at the other three and grin. Outrigger is a four-armed octopus with each of us offering expertise from our different viewpoints.

When we have our assignments, I go into my office and call to update the mayor and police chief. But they brush me off and say it won't be a big deal.

The mayor chuckles. "I'm sure no one is going to come to our little town to get press. We're known as a tourist destination. Not a mecca for picket lines."

The police chief says, "I've got to run. Keep your eyes open and let me know if you learn anything else. We don't think it's anything to worry about. It'll be a few stragglers on the streets, and they'll drift away. The reporters won't care. No one will get violent. Who cares if they sing a few peace songs?"

I hang up thinking it smells to me like poor police command and rigid thinking, but I ignore it and get on with my business. I have a client to attend to.

I text Brinker to set up a meeting today, in an hour, if possible. But ten minutes later, I haven't heard back. I call his office.

"I'm sorry," his assistant says, "but he's taking time off.

He's at his cabin in the woods and told me not to disturb him for any reason unless it was an emergency."

I suppress a slew of swear words that come to mind and bite my lip.

"This is an emergency," I say. "Protesters are already in town and preparing to disrupt normal business operations at your company. I need to speak with him as soon as possible."

"I'll pass your request along if he calls in," she says in a calm voice.

Everyone is acting like a dark cloud isn't hovering over us and about to dump hail the size of golf balls. What do I have to do to convince people this is a real, actual threat?

Keeping my voice even and friendly, I say, "Would you please at least tell employees there not to wear clothing with a company logo for the next two weeks? If they do, that could make them targets for violence or altercations."

"I'm not authorized to act in that capacity," she says.

I squint at the wall and grip the phone tighter. "I see. What did you say your name was?"

"Lydia. Lydia Barker."

"Listen, Lydia, I appreciate any help you can give me during the lead up to the trade association meeting. We need to fend off potential incidents. You know, nip them in the bud before they get started and extinguish the flames?" She's quiet, so I add, "Not add oxygen to the fire?"

"I wouldn't know about that," she says. "I just started here, and I'm working part-time. I'm going to study business at the local college, and I hope to move up the ranks here someday."

"Lydia, I need your help, and I can tell you the sooner you wake up and realize we've got a potential catastrophe on the horizon, the better. You can play a part to prevent it. It's part of doing business. Consider it a hands-on course in crisis management. Just let Mr. Brinker know I need to talk with him in the next hour. You can call me anytime, night or day. I'll email him now to give him an update."

"I'm not sure he's checking his texts or emails. He said he's overdue for a few days off, and his family needs to see him. They deserve to get his sole attention before the big trade association meeting. It's on Monday, is that right?"

Blood pulses in my ears. "Yes, we have three days before all hell breaks loose. We need to prepare."

"Good luck," she says and hangs up.

I slap a palm to my forehead. My team will work over the weekend and have an airtight disaster preparedness plan. We'll get it done. Somehow though, despite attending the protester's planning meeting, I suspect I only have a glimmer of what's to come.

WE HUNKER DOWN and work all weekend at Outrigger, bringing in donuts from The Doughnut House in the morning, with a glazed buttermilk for me, an éclair for Mimi, a chocolate-covered bear claw for Vincent and a blueberry muffin for Flora. We have pizza at noon and Thai take-out for dinner.

When Sunday evening rolls around, my team and I have the situation covered as much as was possible. I haven't heard a peep from Brinker all weekend, and he hasn't responded to my texts or emails. Figures. The poor guy finally takes time off to be with family, and then Armageddon blows into town.

"Tomorrow is Monday," I say to my staff. "Go home and get a good night's rest. The marathon starting gun will go off tomorrow."

6

———————

The next day, I roll out of my cot in my office at five a.m. and go for a run to clear my head. Sitting and working inside while eating carbs isn't the best way to treat my body. I need to be strong and alert to get through the next couple days.

I'm jogging past three people huddled around a camp stove on a sidewalk when I glance down Commercial. Overnight while I slept, a town of tents sprang up on the sidewalks. I swallow hard. The mayor and police chief aren't going to like this.

My phone dings with a text from one of my staff, reminding me of a hot topics meeting in two hours. I think about calling my mother because she's an early riser. Instead, because I'm ticked off with her, I tuck the phone in my pocket. We worked hard over the weekend, and I didn't call her, which was unusual.

The truth is, although I'm tough on the job, I'm afraid to confront my mom. What do you say to a loved one who sells you out and exposes where you live so protesters can swarm your home? The word unforgiveable comes to mind.

Right then, my mom texts me, as if she knew I was thinking about her. We talk most days of the week while I'm warming down after my morning run.

Her text says, "Time for a quick chat? Or are you running?"

I call her back to see if I can glean tidbits of intel from her about the upcoming protest. But if she tries to pry details out of me, I'll be a closed door.

I know how to keep a secret, like the fact that Dad fathered another child with a woman in town. I haven't had the courage yet to email or call the other daughter, but I know she lives here. As far as I know, my mom has no idea, and I'll keep it that way for her sake.

I say, "I was just starting my run. How are you? And did you go on that trip yet?"

"I'm fine, sweetheart. And I haven't left the farm yet. Just lolling around, tending to the vegetables. My life is very boring. You have no idea."

I eye a low-hanging dark cloud over the water and wonder why she's fibbing. What would she gain by pretending she wasn't in the area where I live?

"Really?" I say. "Because I saw someone who looks and

sounds just like you in Millersville the other day. I could've sworn it was you."

She chortles. "You caught me, love. I thought I'd be incognito and slip in and out of town, and you wouldn't notice. I'm here, staying with a group at the Fidalgo RV Resort. I don't have time to get together with you while I'm here, and I apologize. We're busy working on a project. I'll tell you about it when it's over."

I won't tell her I attended the protesters meeting, because if I did, her group would know we have an advantage and inside information. I frown. I need to put off confronting her about how she jeopardized my safety and made herself look better by giving my home address and throwing me under the bus.

Wanting to learn about their plans, I say, "Are you involved in the protest that's going to happen in Millersville? Tell me about it."

She says in a hurried, tight voice, "I've got to go. The group is leaving. Love you. Talk to you later."

I stash my phone in a pocket and glance at Hat Island in the distance, beyond the marina. I'm an isolated island. My mother put her fervent beliefs in a cause ahead of protecting my safety.

I let out a disgusted whoosh of breath and realize I'm more hurt than angry about it. Resting a foot on a bench by the marina, I stretch my legs and focus my mind, letting my personal life fade away.

Nothing matters right now but running. Next up, I'll

shift to work and protecting our client. I'll deal with my feelings when the trade meetings end.

Pumping my legs, I run as fast as I can along the water and down to Seafarer's Memorial. Dawn is breaking by the time I reach a beach tucked behind the breakwater, and I stop, opening my arms wide. I hope my company can survive the raging tempest that is blowing into town.

As I jog back to the office, Brinker calls my cell phone.

I pick up and say, "Good to hear from you. Are you back in town? We need to meet."

"I'm on my way, but we're caught in traffic."

I raise my eyebrows. We don't have traffic jams in our area, except at three in the afternoon when the refinery shift ends. Go near the roundabout then, and you'll have to wait your turn in a long line.

He says, "It's the oddest thing. A bunch of camper vans and pickups with over cabs are heading into Millersville. It's like a wagon train with cars. I'm glad we hired you."

"Sir, I think we have a problem. A big one."

Right then, a line of motorcycles race by, heading downtown. They rev their engines and stop at a corner, popping wheelies. They're big guys with tattoos, wearing black leather jackets and pants and boots. These are not men to mess with.

"What's that?" Brinker says. "Reception cut out. I couldn't hear what you said."

That's typical of our area. Spotty reception unless you have a certain carrier that starts with a letter toward the end of the alphabet. I had my team do a comparison test with various cell phone carriers at our previous company. We picked the one with the most consistent coverage, because we need to be ready at all times to respond.

I draw a breath and pray for patience. "I said, the situation is turning into what looks to be a negative one. We've got motorcyclists swarming the streets. "

A bunch of Harleys blast past, about twenty of them, but I'm not taking time to do an exact count.

"Can you repeat that?" Brinker says.

"When you get back to the office, text me and I'll come over. We've got people camping on Commercial, motorcyclists coming into town and protesters are organizing. They're smart and prepared, and they're going to be a mighty adversary."

The cell signal drops.

"Hello?" I say.

But no one is there.

7

———

Back at the office, I take a quick shower in the women's room. Mimi bikes to work, and we run during lunch as a pack sometimes, so I made sure to have facilities where we could clean up and change clothes. As a group we're exercise fiends and committed to staying in shape.

Brinker texts when I reach my desk. "Ready to meet when you are. Come over as soon as you can."

"OK," I text back. "See you soon."

I walk to his building and mull over what's ahead. The trade association meetings start this afternoon, and we're nowhere near ready. I need to brief Brinker, give his staff a heads up, and scramble back to the team to get updates from their reconnaissance.

I march into Brinker's office after breezing past his assistant. It's great he's offering part-time work to Lydia. I wonder if the police have spoken with her about the threatening letter, and the envelope it came in.

In his office, I say, "Did the police talk to Lydia yet about the threat she opened that came in the mail?"

"I don't believe so, but I've been out of town as you know."

When I turn to go back and speak with Lydia, he says, "That's not Lydia out there. Her name is Colleen. She has a child in elementary school and only wants to work mornings."

I sit down on a straight back upholstered chair covered in a maroon fabric. "Okay, good to know. Let's get started. Are you aware that protesters are in town, and they've talked about targeting your company?"

His eyebrows shoot up, and he shakes his head. "No, I hadn't heard that. This concerns me. You should've let me know how serious the situation was before now."

I sigh. "I tried texting and emailing you, but you didn't respond. And Lydia refused to pass along a message about the urgency of the situation. She said you wanted time away with your family at a cabin?"

He leans back in his executive black chair, and it creaks. "We rarely get out there. We've got a little cabin along the slough. The kids love going there and making bonfires, roasting marshmallows, telling stories by the campfire."

"I understand. It sounds great. Kids love to spend time with their families, until they get older, that is."

I think back to when I was young and the outings my mom and dad and I had heading to the Washington Coast. Once I found a dead seal. The stench filled my nostrils and made me gag. At night, we stayed at a cabin in Kalaloch. We'd face west and watch wild waves crash on shore while telling spooky ghost stories. Until Dad left, that is.

Clearing my throat, I say, "I'd like to brief your senior staff and communications team. I also suggest you email your employees and tell them to work from home during the meetings, and not to wear clothing items with the company logo until the protesters leave town."

"I'll do that," he says, pushing up a cuticle. "No need for you to bill me for talking to my staff. We agreed you'd bill me by the hour, isn't that right?"

I nod.

"How much are we up to now? What's the ballpark bill?"

I name a fee that makes his jaw drop. "That's a rough estimate, given we've been on this since you and I last met, and working over the weekend."

He says, "I hope it's worth it. For that amount, I could've hired an in-house person to handle it."

"They wouldn't have our background, sir. My staff and I are experienced in preventing corporate crises and that gives us superior skills as a response team. Our motto is: Assess, prevent, and exit. Besides, by using Outrigger, there's more of us to provide updates and keep you informed, instead of you relying on one inside person."

He grunts. "Fine. You tell a good story. I only hope it's money well spent."

I wish he'd let me speak directly to his staff to convey how dire the situation is, but it's his company, and he's the client. This may be the case of where the client is not always right. I hope it won't bite me in the butt later, and I won't lose my first client.

"Understood. Tell your people no flashy logo lanyards. No showing employee badges outside this facility, and no baseball caps with logos. I want them to be heads down and invisible, blending in with pedestrians gathering in the streets. We don't want a protester to rip off an employee badge and gain access to the building. They could shut your servers down."

"Aren't you going a bit overboard? It's only a trade association steering committee meeting."

"The thing is, sir, it doesn't sound or smell or look like 'just a meeting.' I attended a protesters' planning meeting in disguise the other day while you were out of town. They aim to disrupt Millersville and your company with the goal of gaining local and national media attention."

He growls. His face is grim and pale. "Let them try to come after us. We'll flick them off like flies. We've got you on our side. You'll protect us."

"You bet," I say, but inside, I'm quaking. "We can't predict with certainty how people will act in the coming days. There's a small chance that even with foresight and preparation, this could get out of control."

I gesture to the door. "I'll check the conference room downstairs before I leave."

"That's a good idea. Let me know if you find anything."

8

____

I search the meeting room for listening devices and surveillance cameras, looking under the table and in light fixtures, and find none. Business people file into the room, and I leave. From what I've heard, they're millionaires and billionaires, but they're wearing jeans and sneakers and casual clothes. It's their perfect haircuts that give their wealth away. Each woman and man taking a place at the conference table has a precision cut that only money can buy.

Outside the building is a different story. A crowd is forming in front of Bettermed. They have built a make-shift stage. On it, the tall leader from the protest planning meeting stands next to a woman holding a microphone.

I march outside to get a better look. The woman leads a chant. When I sidle closer, I finch. It's my mother.

"What do we want?" Daisy shouts, waving an arm.

"Freedom," people in sweatshirts and rain jackets say, raising clenched fists.

Rain drizzles down, peppering us with unwelcome moisture. Perhaps the group will disperse given the inclement weather. A breeze kicks up, making my mom's long hair fly around her face. She pushes it away and holds the microphone to her mouth.

If this crowd is as determined as Daisy is, the town of Millersville is in for the fight of our lives. Who knows how it'll look on the other side, after the trade meetings are over.

Daisy says, "Will we allow Big Brother to listen to us?"

"Hell, no," the crowd answers.

"Do we want server farms harming the environment?"

"No, we don't," the crowd yells.

"That's right," my mom says, nodding and smiling. "No. More. Server. Farms."

The crowd echoes her words. "No. More. Server. Farms."

Daisy says, "Protect the environment."

"Protect the environment,"

"Protect Mother Earth," my dear mother says.

"Protect Mother Earth."

She hands the microphone to the tall leader.

He says, "Now it's time for our drum circle. We'll parade down Commercial at noon."

About fifteen women and men of all ages with tall drums and bongo drums step on the stage and sit in a circle. One woman taps out a beat, bop, de bop, de bop, and the others follow. The sound bounces off walls of downtown buildings.

My mom steps down off the stage, and people surge around her, clapping her on the back. I'll talk with her later. But I doubt she'll listen to me or change her mind. She is one for a cause. It's just changed from volunteering at the hospital and at the senior center to saving the earth and working on a farm.

I nod to Vincent, who is covering the front entrance, and head around to the back door. I've got to keep my client foremost in my mind instead of being distracted by Daisy.

A woman in tight jeans, ankle boots, and a black leather jacket approaches the building. She doesn't strike me as being a protester. She shoulders past bystanders and steps to the back entrance.

She smiles at me with perfect white teeth. "I'm here for the trade association meeting."

Something about her strikes me as odd. She might be an interloper in disguise, trying to gain access to disrupt the meeting inside.

"Credentials?" I say.

Her jaw drops. "Pardon me?"

"I'd like to see your identification."

She shakes her head. "I'm not going to show you that. Just open the door. I'm going inside."

From the way she sets her jaw, she's either a true trade

association member and totally ticked off. Or, she's acting a good part.

"Hold on," I say and motion to my second-in-command, Mimi, who is standing there.

"What'd you think?" I say in a low voice.

"My call is she doesn't belong. I saw her get out of an older model van. Not something I'd say a software executive would drive."

"Got it." I turn to the now frowning woman, who is rummaging through her purse. "Show us a business card with your name on it and photo ID, please. We're ensuring the safety of people inside the building."

She plucks out a driver's license and business card. "There, satisfied?"

Mimi examines them. "Looks good."

The woman tucks them back in her big bag of a purse. "The rental car company said that old van was all they had left, given the number of people that were coming into town."

"Our apologies for delaying you," I say. I badge open the door and hold it open.

"I need to talk to someone named Violet," she says, striding in. "Do you know who that is?"

I raise my eyebrows. "That's me."

I hold out my hand to shake, but she wrinkles her nose.

"I'm Belinda, and I'll be in touch with you later. You haven't made the best first impression."

As she stalks inside, I turn to Mimi. "What's your assessment of the situation?"

"Fine for now, but with the number of people milling about, anything could happen. My source at the police says they're not ready to control the crowd if it gets out of hand. They haven't discussed what they'd do, and they lack the equipment and staff to mount a response."

I scratch my cheek. "In that case, I hope it's a peaceful protest, not an incendiary event."

The drums go silent. From the opposite side of the building, I hear Daisy's voice, blasting through a megaphone and telling people to walk peacefully down the street. I've got to admit I admire her for taking a visible leadership role. She shook off the wall flower she was when I was growing up and has stepped out into her own. If she wasn't on opposite sides of the protest in town, I'd be cheering her on. Go, Mom, go. No, wait, leave town, Mom. And don't come back.

I hustle to the front of the building just in time to see Daisy in a yellow caftan marching down Commercial Avenue, leading a parade. She repeats the chants I heard earlier, and the crowd shouts back, in a call and response.

Daisy says, "Will we let Big Brother make our choices?"

"Hell, no," people say.

"Do we want server farms harming the environment?"

"No, we don't," the crowd yells.

"Protect the environment."

"Protect the environment,"

"Protect Mother Earth."

"Protect Mother Earth."

Feet pound the pavement. The ground trembles. Two people go by carrying a huge banner that says, "Stop the Meetings. Protect the Sacred Trust."

A man dressed as a turtle goes by, accompanied by a woman in a dolphin costume. They hold up picket signs. "Save the earth. Stop server farms." Another sign says, "No to big brother. We decide for ourselves."

All kinds of people are here. Old and young. Women and men with babies in front carriers, and kids on their shoulders. People in tie dye shirts with sweatpants and others in button-down shirts and jeans march down the street.

A line of drummers file past, slapping hands on drums hung around their necks. The beat repeats, and I find myself tapping a foot to the catchy rhythm. This isn't so bad, I tell myself. They're making their views known in a respectful manner. Covering this event will be a breeze, and it'll be over in a flash. Why was I so worried?

A woman in her early thirties with curly brown hair stops to tie the shoelace of her orange sneaker.

"Hello," I say, going up to her to learn more, "can I ask why you're here? What's the appeal?"

Her eyes open wide. "Don't you know? This is the most important protest the country will see this year.

We're coming out in force to support our sisters and brothers in the fight."

I tilt my head. "And what's the fight about? I see all kinds of signs with different messages. I'm not sure if you're all here for the same reason."

She grins. "We're not, and it doesn't matter that we all come from different vantage points. We're here to take part, so we can tell our friends and our kids one day that we were part of the Millersville Protest. It's going to be like Woodstock, you know? Where only those who were at the festival really knew what it was like and got to tell others about it later. There will never be another protest like this, if we pull it off like we intend to."

"You sound passionate about your cause. By the way, could I have your name and phone number, in case a reporter wants to contact you later?" I'm fibbing, but I want an inside source to call if I need it, other than my mother.

She tucks her hair behind her ears. "Sure, I'd love to speak with the press. I work for a nature preservation non-profit, and I'm here to gather support and gain new followers on social media."

She gives me her number and says her name is Martina.

"And who are you?" she says, staring into my eyes.

I use all my training not to look away, or squirm, or cross my arms. If I'm defensive, she might rat me out as being from the other side. I imagine a group surrounding me, shouting my name and poking fingers at me for representing the establishment and protecting the bad guy in town. I don't want attention. I just want to blend in and gather data.

I shrug. "I'm nobody, really, just a curious bystander appreciating the spectacle."

She says, "It'll be even better tomorrow, when more people will join us."

She turns to go, but I reach out and touch her elbow. "Did you say more people are on the way?"

"Yep, we have busloads coming from SeaTac airport. Teamsters and Communications Workers of America and United Farm Workers and supporters are flying in from all over the country." She raises her hands as if she's in an evangelical church. "Just wait, tomorrow will be bigger and better. We'll send a message that will be heard like a thunderclap all over the world."

I gulp. This sounds bad. But I'm glad I learned about it now, instead of being surprised tomorrow. "Nice talking with you," I say.

She sets off, joining a stream of people flowing past.

I cuss under my breath. I've got to brief Brinker, the police chief, and the mayor so they can call in reinforcements and set up barricades. If not, the protests for the STA meetings might spin out of control.

9

———————

Back at my office, I text the mayor and police chief to give them an update. When neither of them responds, I call their offices. I shake my head. If this is how they're acting today, how will the rest of the week go?

If I were them, I'd be on call and reachable at any moment. My job calls for me to be ready to hit the ground running at a moment's notice. But not everyone lives like I do.

This state of constant readiness hasn't done my body any favors. My heightened alert response probably is what led to a benign tumor in my right adrenal gland. When the endocrinologist diagnosed me with a rare condition last year, I groaned. I wanted to go back to work, not get robotic surgery.

Anyway, I recovered just fine and was walking hours

after surgery, doing laps around the hospital halls and the nursing station. But the end effect is I tend to baby myself a bit more now. I try not to get stressed out by little things.

But my mom being here and stirring up a fuss isn't helping me keep a zen state of mind. She's rattling my cage quite a bit. I lean over and take a few slow breaths, sipping salty sea air wafting past. Breathe in, breathe out, and let it go. This will pass in a few days. I'll do just fine. My client will be pleased. Word will get out and Outrigger will attract more clients from this job.

The mayor's assistant picks up her line. "Mayor's office. How may I help you?"

I say, "I need to speak with the mayor right away. Something's come up."

"I'm sorry, she's out of the office and unavailable."

My brows furrow. "When do you expect her in?"

"Not for a few days. She's at a charity golf event for a children's foundation."

My hand holding the cell phone shakes. "A few days?"

"Yes, it's been on the calendar for a year, and she made a commitment to attend. She said it wouldn't look good if she was to cancel at the last minute."

"Listen, it's absolutely urgent. If you speak to her, tell her to call me. I'll text and email her too. Crowds are gathering in the street, and bus loads more are coming into town tomorrow. It might turn into egg on our face, and I need help to calm things down."

"Sounds serious," she says.

"It is. I'll call the police chief and let him know what's going on too."

"Oh, he's at the same golf tournament. By the way, I heard they were told to put their phones in a lock box before playing golf and attending a dinner tonight. And tomorrow too. It's part of the ground rules they agreed to when they signed up and donated money."

"Where exactly is the tournament being held? Maybe I'll go speak to them myself."

"Oh, I don't think that's possible. It's over in Eastern Washington in a country club. They'll be back the day after tomorrow though," she says in an upbeat voice.

I blow out a breath. "Thanks for your help. I'll be in touch. If the mayor calls, tell her crowd control is a concern, and tomorrow it'll escalate."

"Kay, bye then, have a nice day."

I hang up and lean against the wall of my office for support. I check in with Mimi, who agrees I should call the police and tell them what I heard. She gives me the name and number of the officer who is second in command.

I dial and wait on hold for five minutes.

A woman comes on the line. She sounds ticked off right from the start of the conversation. "How can I help you?"

"I'm Violet Cleveland, and I own Outrigger Services."

"Yeah, the company who charges for what the public gets for free from us."

"We could debate that later, but I wanted to give the police a heads up that tomorrow busloads of protesters are coming from SeaTac Airport. There'll be a lot more people in town, and I suspect things may get rowdy or dangerous. We'll need crowd control."

"We've had discussions here and decided that won't be necessary. The protesters aren't harming anyone, and they have a permit for gathering in a public place."

"Okay, well, if you could just pass it along to the others, so they're prepared in case things turn sideways."

"We've got it under control, don't you worry," she says. "Your public police force at work, serving the people. We're on top of it."

"I'll fill you in with updates if I hear anything more."

"No need for that. We've got officers in cars monitoring the streets."

"But the cars might not be able to get through tomorrow, what with the crowds they're expecting. We need officers on foot and eyes on the ground."

"We'll be the judge of that, thank you." With a click, she hangs up.

I let out a whistle. That didn't go well. I type out text messages to the mayor and police chief: "New intel: busloads of protesters arriving tomorrow. Situation may escalate. Suggest you return to town."

I send the messages and set down my phone, striding to the main room.

"Let's gather round for a meeting. I have an update,

and I want to hear what you've learned."

10

———————

The next morning, I yawn and stretch in my office. It's Tuesday, and I have the feeling it's a make-or-break day. Whatever happens will prove whether we have a peaceful protest going on or one that needs police presence. I slept in a t-shirt and shorts, so I only have to pull on my socks and shoes and grab a sweatshirt to go for a run.

Outside, the air is crisp and clean. I take a deep breath of the briny air and am glad once more that fate brought me to this small town in the Pacific Northwest, which happens to have the highest rate of boat ownership in the entire U.S.

Jogging past The Depot on the way to the marina and the trail that goes along Padilla Bay, I stop when I hear voices inside.

I creep over to the open door and lean my shoulder against the wall of the decommissioned old rail station.

"I've called reporters," a man with a deep voice says, "and let them know to show up tomorrow morning at Bettermed at the front entrance. Two TV stations and a Seattle newspaper said they'll cover the press conference. We'll start at eight, so it can hit the morning news cycle."

A woman says, "With crowds building today, and people marching, it'll be a perfect lead into tomorrow's activities."

My muscles tense. Adrenaline kicks in. My hands fist.

I turn and shuffle away before the protesters see me lingering and loitering. Letting out pent up energy, I fly past the marina and down the Tommy Thompson trail. I've got wings on my feet from facing fear.

By the time I turn back to the office, my body is spent, and my mind is calm. I'm ready to oversee a critical defense of Mr. B's company, with the support of my staff.

I rush into the shower, soap up and wash down, and in fifteen minutes, I'm at my desk. Tapping a pen against the desk top, I come up with a plan to foil the protesters' press conference tomorrow morning. I made a few calls, interrupting trades people having their morning coffee, and email my plan to my client.

Within minutes, he responds. "Excellent plan. Looking forward to see how it works out tomorrow morning. I'll tell employees to stay home or use the back entrance."

Mimi comes into work. Her hair is damp. Her cheeks are rosy.

"Morning, boss."

"Morning. Anything new out there since I came back from my run?"

She nods. "A bunch of old RVs and run down campers are parked on two side streets, blocking access to downtown. Pedestrians can still get through though. I left my car a few blocks away and walked here."

"Good to know. How are we for working with the police on crowd control?"

She says, "They say they have barricades, but they're stored off premises in a warehouse out by La Conner."

I raise my eyebrows. "Do they think if needed they can go get them and bring them back in time? What if they can't drive into downtown when the busloads of people arrive today?"

"I know, if I were in charge, I'd place the barricades on the streets, in case they're needed, so they can be moved into place in an instant. My contact at the police wouldn't say how many they had. She said the optics wouldn't be good if they put the barriers out now. The mayor wants our town to look approachable to visitors. The TV coverage would be negative if we looked ready to fight these peaceful people."

I say, "Is this small town living or what? I'd rather they were prepared for the worst and hope for the best outcome. But they've got their heads in the sand."

She crosses her arms. "We've seen this before, and we know what to do." She breaks into a wide grin. "At least we know what we're doing and how to protect Bettermed. Thank goodness we're not responsible for defending the whole town."

"With eighteen thousand residents living here and what looks like near a thousand protesters gathering with more on the way, we may need to step up our game and dampen the flames. It's becoming a bigger ask than what the initial contract said."

"I hear you," she says.

I pick up my phone and keys. "Listen, I need to step out and get some clothes from my place. Take charge while I'm gone, okay?"

Mimi turns to the window, and I join her.

"Doesn't look good, does it?" she says.

Commercial is packed with people, and it's not even nine in the morning.

"It could go either way," I say.

But deep in my heart, I know when you get tons of people pressed together, violence is more likely to break out. All it takes is one half-cocked angry person to light the match.

This is going to be one heck of a day. And night. And the next day.

11

I hustle past stragglers on the street, grouped in clumps of two or three or five. Their hoodies are pulled up, and it's hard to see their faces. From the way they're shuffling their feet, they look like they're waiting for someone to round them up. But then again, maybe I'm being paranoid. This whole thing could blow over, and the mayor and police chief will have a laugh at my expense, toasting to each other after the protesters leave town.

I hop in my RAV-4 and drive to my house to pick up clothes for the next few days. Tents are set up on sidewalks and in parks. Come on, mayor and police chief, get back to town so you'll have eyes on the ground. You need to see what's going on in your own town.

I pull up to my two-bedroom turquoise blue bungalow and park on the street, killing the engine. In the driveway is an older model VW camper van painted with flowers. The lights are on inside the house, and I didn't leave it that way.

My stomach churns. The painted camper van is my mother's. I rest a hand on my belly and remind myself to skip the extra doughnut when I get back to the office.

Why is my relative the one who is a budding protest leader? I wish she'd stayed on her farm and not come into town, stirring up trouble.

I climb out and lock the car door. My neighborhood is safe, but I don't trust Daisy or her friends not to hop in my car and riffle through the contents, looking for cash or valuables to pawn. Anything is possible in our relationship from here on out. We entered uncharted territory when she told the group where I live, and she risked my life.

Moving with stealth to the front door, which is ajar, I pause and listen.

A woman says in a nasal voice, "Your daughter sure doesn't keep much food in the house, does she? We were counting on being able to make sandwiches for people waiting at The Depot."

Daisy laughs. "Violet never was the homebody type after high school. She was always off flitting around the globe when she was in the military. But she never told me where she was going, or what she did when she was there. I just knew I couldn't reach her, and my texts didn't go through sometimes for a week or more."

My hands clench. My fingernails bite into my palms. She shouldn't be sharing private information about my past.

"Wait," a man says in a deep voice. "Are you saying your daughter is ex-military? She and her team might pose more of a threat than we thought at the outset. I had them marked down as amateurs defending a local software company."

My mom mumbles, and I can't make out what she says.

I barge in so fast, the front door slams into the wall.

"Mom," I say, striding in. "This is my house. What're you doing here uninvited?"

I glare at the three of them and scan the kitchen.

A woman in her early thirties who is digging in a mayonnaise jar turns to me. She opens her mouth and stares. A knife in her hand clatters to the floor, spraying droplets of white on the gray tile.

I put my hands on my hips and glare.

A man with a long brown beard scratches his chin. He's sitting at the round kitchen table, assembling sandwiches with my Bread Farm whole wheat bread that tastes out of this world. He squirts yellow mustard on slabs of bread. Then he sets the plastic container down with a thump and sits back, crossing his arms. He looks me in the eye.

I glare back, having just met my newest adversary. What a jackass, sitting in my home like he owns it and eating my food. His body language screams, "Just try and fuck with me. You'll regret it."

My mom is wearing jeans and an orange sweatshirt. Her long hair is wet, and I bet she used my shower. She leans against the counter, and her chest heaves with short breaths. She looks nervous, and I bet it's because I've caught her out.

I didn't give my mother a key to this house intentionally. The last place I lived she came through and had a party with people she met on a hiking trail. They trashed the place. Beer cans left on every surface, dripping and stinking up the place. Butts of marijuana joints in ash trays, tipped over on the floor. Burns in my pretty red pillows picked out from Target.

Daisy studies the floor.

"Mom, what're you doing here?"

I glance around for an entry point. They didn't come in through the front door, because that's intact. My heart thumps when I spot the broken living room window.

"Really?" I say, "You broke my window? Breaking and entering at your daughter's place, what're you thinking? I'll call the police."

I whip out my phone. I really don't want to report my mom and have her locked up in jail. After all, she is my mother.

She rushes over. "We didn't mean to break the window, but there was no other way in. You didn't give me a key like you used to, or leave one under a flowerpot, or over the door. What were we supposed to do? I needed to take a long, hot shower. I was desperate."

I clench my jaw. It's all about Daisy, the never-ending show. I clamp my lips shut and keep quiet to see what else she has to say for herself.

She gestures to the two others. "And they wanted a hot shower too, without paying for it at the campground. I'm sick of staying in a tent. Can we stay with you tonight?"

I snort. "That's a strange request after you trashed my last place and broke in here. I can't believe you expected to be invited back? Remember the burn marks in the wall-to-wall carpet? I had to pay to replace that."

Putting her hands together as if in prayer, she blinks at me and says, "Please?"

I snort and purse my lips. How many times has she tried this act? Two? Or more? I've lost count.

She tilts her head and stares with big brown eyes, pleading for my forgiveness. Asking for me to open my home and welcome her, despite her past transgressions and proven poor judgement.

I frown. After my dad left, she announced she didn't want to spend another minute of her life doing house-keeping chores. She kept her word and went way overboard. I wonder what my bathroom looks like. Probably slob-city, like a storm blew through.

A thought crosses my mind. Who is the mother here, and who is the child? Since my dad left, she's come to depend on me for money, for stability, for whatever she needs and whenever she wants it. When she asked for the security deposit and first and last on her first apartment when she moved away from our family home, I paid it. She left for the farm after that without cleaning the place, leaving trash and pizza boxes and old clothes. I never saw the money again.

I tell myself to buck up and be strong in the face of Daisy's requests. Don't give in. Change the dynamic. But I've dug a hole for myself by taking care of my mom's emotional, financial, and physical needs.

That's why I was relieved when she moved to The Farm with a group of people. I'd hoped she'd get the support she needed there and rely less on me. But here she is in Millersville and right here in my home, mucking up my personal and professional life.

I grab a whole wheat cheese sandwich and stuff it in my jacket pocket. The bread is too good to let it leave the house without my taking some.

Gesturing to the open front door, I say, "Go on, clear out. Take the sandwiches with you, and don't come back. If you weren't family, I'd have called the police by now. I don't want to see you on my property ever again."

I give my mom a harsh look and point to the other two culprits. "If there is a next time, and I see you on my property, I'll conduct a citizen's arrest. You'll regret breaking in and opening my frig, eating anything you see in sight."

I whip out my phone and snap pictures of each of them. They stare and look like deer in the headlights. Or more like angry convicts headed to jail, which is where they'll be if I find them inside my house a second time. I snap a photo of the broken window for proof of what they did.

"Am I clear?"

They nod.

"Understood?"

"Yeah," my mom says in a soft voice. She saves that quiet tone to pair with her penitent look of remorse when she's done something wrong, and I'm out money. Good grief, she's like a teenager, calling me to pick her up after causing an accident.

They don't budge from the kitchen, so I point to the front door. "Out."

Mom raises her hands. "But Ralph hasn't taken his shower yet."

"I don't care. You and your group are not welcome in my house. In the future, don't come inside, and don't camp in my yard. If you do, you'll regret it."

The man named Ralph pulls out a gun and aims it at me.

My pulse quickens. My armpits prickle with sweat. I put a hand on my holster and spread my legs apart, standing my ground.

I wait for my mother to say something. If she loved me, she'd intervene and protect me. My mom is silent.

He says, "Is this what you want? Really? To turn your mother away?"

Locking eyes with Ralph, I say, "That's my gun, isn't it?"

I'm speaking in a calm voice. I don't want to rattle him or have the 9-millimeter Glock go off by accident and hit someone.

He nods. "Found it upstairs in the bedroom when I was looking around."

I stifle the urge to scream. No one breaks into my house and takes my things. I won't let the situation escalate, but it takes all my self-control not to shoot him in the knees. My mother and the other woman are standing close to him and might get hit. I can't let innocent bystanders and my relative get hurt.

I left my gun in my bedside table, and it's my fault some idiot found it to use against me. I should've put it in the safe. It's partly my fault I'm in this predicament.

He smiles and looks like he's enjoying the attention and power of aiming a weapon at an innocent homeowner. His hands shake, and he's holding it with both hands. But lucky for me, the gun isn't loaded. I keep the ammo in a separate place.

He can't hurt me unless he bludgeons me with it. I eye his civilian's soft body. I could overtake him. He might not realize it, but I could kill him, if I whipped out my holstered weapon and fired.

But there's no need to escalate the situation. I don't have time to call the police to report a crime and whine about being threatened. What I want is for my mother and her friends to leave, so I can go back to work downtown.

"Put the gun down and go," I say. "If you do, I won't hurt you."

My mom says to Ralph, "What're you thinking? Set it on the table and walk away. We're peaceful people. We don't believe in guns. Not like my darling daughter does."

I raise an eyebrow at her tone. She's never liked the need for weapons in my line of work. If she hated the military so much, why did she marry my dad? But I know the answer to that. He was charming as all get out and he carried a tune and played the guitar. She fell in love with his voice, and the same was true for me. A memory of a family sing-along in the back yard comes to me before I shake my head to clear it away.

Taking a slow breath, I vow not to let her get under my skin.

"Nice and easy, Ralph," I say. "No swift motions. Just set it down and walk away."

Ralph places the gun on the wood table. He stands and jams the sandwiches into one of my coolers I store in the laundry room. They certainly have helped themselves to my belongings and made themselves at home.

"Get the jugs of water, Daisy," he says.

"Yep." She nods to me as she traipses past carrying two of my earthquake preparedness jugs of bottled water. They are heavy, but I'm not about to help her.

She calls to the younger woman in the kitchen, "Millie, let's go. Time to scram. My daughter doesn't want to share her home with us. How's that for hospitality from a family member?"

As they file out, I say, "You better believe me when I say next time, I won't go as easy on the three of you. You can take that to the RV park and make a bumper sticker saying it. Tattoo it on your foreheads, so you'll remember. Don't come back."

As they amble to the van, Daisy says, "I don't really like my daughter and never could rely on her or my ex-husband. They're both too self-centered. Wouldn't a good daughter welcome you into their home and invite you and your friends to stay over?"

Ralph says, "She'll wake up and so will the whole town when we make our voices heard at the protest downtown."

I close and lock the door. The dead bolt slides into place with a satisfying click. I lean against it, clenching and unclenching my fists, and blow out a hot angry breath. Doesn't she see how she is or acts in the world? She expects me to take care of her, and I'm fed up with it. It's about time I stood up for myself and stopped bending like a willow branch, going into debt to cover her mistakes.

Like the time she asked me to co-sign on a car loan, and I agreed. She wrecked the car and defaulted on the loan and who was stuck paying the rest? Little old sucker me, the daughter with a paying job. Just because I like my work doesn't mean she can expect me to hand her money as a relative.

In the bathroom, water puddles on the tile floor. Thanks, Mom. Another thing to mop up after she visited in the saga of my life.

I wipe up the floor with a towel and brush a tear from my cheek. My own mother said she doesn't like me? That hurts, deep in my heart. I always suspected as much, but now I have confirmation. I thought it was all in my head.

Someone knocks on the door and rings the doorbell.

I step to the side and say through the door, "Who is it?"

Ralph says, "Our van didn't start. Do you have jumper cables?"

I shake my head. "I'm fresh out of favors for you and your group. Why don't you push it and jump start it, pop the clutch."

He says, "It's your own mother, for god's sake. Don't you want to make sure she's safe?"

"Really? You're going there? When you and my mom broke into my house?"

I bite my tongue to stop mentioning her exposing me at the protester meeting and telling everyone where I lived and worked. I don't want them to know I was there.

He shuffles away, and his footsteps fade. I step to the front window and peer out as they push the van out of the driveway. It collides with a fire hydrant and comes to a stop. They stand there scratching their heads.

The van moves off a few minutes later, chugging down the street.

I whip the curtains closed and hurry around the house, picking up after the slobs. When the bathroom floor is mopped and the kitchen is spotless, I go out to the garage and grab a piece of plywood. Those suckers aren't climbing in the same way again. Using a power drill, I screw in screws to hold a piece of plywood up over the window. Try getting that off.

I dust my hands off on my pants, grab a set of T-shirts, socks and set out for the office, after locking up. Driving along, I realize I left the gun out, so I turn around and go back, locking it in my gun safe.

If the town wasn't on the verge of being in an uproar, I'd call the police and ask for a drive by to monitor my place for the next two days. But I get the feeling every woman and man in the police force will be needed on hand to quell what looks like an organized rebellion.

12

When I show up at Outrigger Services, Mimi says, "Where've you been? I thought you were just running home to grab some clothes?" She studies my empty hands. "And where are the doughnuts? I thought you were picking them up on the way back?"

I smack my forehead. "I forgot."

"That's okay. It's late enough now, people are hungry for an early lunch. They voted for Subway sandwiches. I'll take care of it."

"The reason I was delayed," I say, "is because my mother and two other people broke in and were in my kitchen making sandwiches, with my Bread Farm bread."

Mimi eyes me. "You love that bread. You drive over to Bow-Edison just to get it. Is that ticking you off as much as your mom breaking into your house?"

I say in a low voice so as not to distract Flora and Vincent, who are typing on their laptops, "I think so. The whole situation has me out of sorts. How am I supposed to act like a professional when my own mother is undermining me?"

Mimi gives me a smile. "But you're the boss. You're the best I've worked with. You can handle it."

Buoyed by her confidence, I say, "Thanks. We can talk more about this later."

I turn to the others and say, "Now where are we? Anything new while I was out?"

Mimi, Vincent and Flora run down what they've learned in the last hour or so.

I nod. "Good, we're making progress. We'll be ready when this whole thing blows up, if it does."

My stomach growls. I'm hungry, and the cheese sandwich in my pocket is calling to me. While I eat, I'd like to confer with my second-in-command. She's a good listener, and I consider her a friend.

I pat her shoulder and say, "Mimi, let's go in my office for a moment."

I close the door and sit in my chair.

She takes a seat.

"I'd say there are over a thousand people in town for this event," I say. "What's your estimate?"

Mimi glances at the ceiling and pauses for a beat. "Twelve to fifteen hundred is my best guess."

"With more on the way in buses." I reach in my pocket

and pull out a mashed cheese sandwich. "I don't need anything from Subway. I'll eat this instead."

Her brow furrows. "Where'd you get that? And why's it in your pocket?"

With my feet on the desk, I go into greater detail about what happened at my place in the last hour.

While I chomp down on the bread, Mimi says, "If it were me, I would've called the cops right away. I wouldn't have given them a warning. No second times for me, not if someone broke into my house."

I swallow and say, "But it's my mother. She's not perfect, but no one is. My family is a bit messed up."

She shrugs. "Whose isn't? We're all damaged in some form or other."

I nod and chew. How right she is.

She says, "Want us run a check on your house tonight while you're busy? Do a few drive-bys?"

"I'd appreciate that. They wanted to stay at my place, but I shot that down. Tell Vincent and Flora to cruise by and look for people camping in my yard. I did not authorize that. No one but me should be in my house or on the property."

She looks ready to stand when I cough up the fur ball.

"My mom is hanging out with a tall guy named Ralph. He went in my bedroom and found a pistol I keep in my bedside drawer. He had the gun in the kitchen, and he pointed it at me. I managed to talk him down."

Talking about the incident makes my pulse pick up.

Ralph doesn't realize how easy I let him off. If my mother hadn't been there, I'd have disarmed him immediately and shoved him to the floor. Her being there clouded my judgement.

I sit back and wonder if I'll be any good at my job this week with my mother in the mix. I'm not sure I can handle the blending of my personal life and past problems with being on the job.

Mimi says, "Whoa, this just got a whole lot more dangerous. Anyone who is willing to point a gun at you is a threat we take seriously. Did you get the gun back?"

"I did, but it took some convincing." A shiver runs through me, and I rub my arms. "I have a bad feeling about this group and this whole event."

She stands and puts a hand on the doorknob. "I do too. When you have a minute, come out and give us a description of this guy. We'll see if we can find anything about his background. I want to know who we're dealing with before it gets out of control."

"I'll be out in a minute."

She leaves, and my phone buzzes with a text from the mayor.

"We came back early but are stuck at the roundabout. Busloads of people are headed to Millersville. They can't all be going to the protest, can they?"

I text back. "Yes, they can. Suggest you put your staff on high alert. Things may get ugly."

"I'll pass it on to the Chief," she replies.

"Tell him officers may need barricades and pepper spray and tear gas."

"Tear gas is a bridge too far," she replies. "We're a nice, clean, friendly town. We welcome visitors. We don't treat them that way. It'd be bad press."

I set down my phone and shake my head. Being nice never works when violence breaks out. My team is trained to contain, distract, and deploy counter-measures. But if the mayor and police chief don't want to assume the worst, let them have their heads-in-the-sand flawed decision making. If we're nice, as the mayor put it, we might be perceived as weak and mowed down by a mob. No telling what'll happen when the bus loads of supporters arrive.

By this afternoon, we may have a different situation on our hands, and protecting the client may become a more difficult task. Our quiet little waterfront town may be about to turn into a battle ground.

13

Drums thunder, and the window panes rattle in our offices. Outrigger Services is just off Commercial, which is the main street in downtown. Brakes screeching and rumbling engines makes me curious, and I get up and go to the window.

Yellow buses clog the streets. They are everywhere I look. Parked at the curb, blocking the street, down by the dog park, and over by the marina.

A sea of people of all ages are climbing off the buses. Many carry picket signs. A woman in her fifties with ash blond hair in a bob holds up a sign that says, "Justice for Jobs." She looks up and waves at me, and I return the gesture.

A young man in his early twenties is frowning. His sign says, "No more layoffs."

I step back from the window and wonder who are the most dangerous members of the public. Is it the fanatics who will stop at nothing to deliver their message? Or the people who have lost work and are angry at tech companies? My team and I will find out in the next two days.

When I go into the bullpen, my staff are at the windows, studying the situation.

"Looks like this is turning real," Mimi says.

"Sure does," I say. "Anybody got a current crowd count? Estimates with the busloads of protesters coming in just now?"

Vincent checks a camera we mounted on the rooftop. "My best guess is two thousand and rising. Traffic cams along Highway 20 show more buses on the way. They're snaking their way into town like slugs clogging the road."

I wipe my forehead. "So, we could end up with three thousand people here in Millersville before the sun sets?"

Mimi nods. "Looks that way to me. Want me to get on the phone with my contact at the police?"

"Yes, and find out what their emergency crisis plan is, so we can work together. Hopefully by now, the police and City Hall are acting on our intelligence."

Five minutes later, Mimi knocks on my door. "Got a minute?"

"Of course, what's up?"

She sinks into a chair. It's beat up and been knocked about, but I don't care. I bought second-hand office furniture to keep the overhead costs down. We're not about looking posh. We care about delivering top-notch security services to corporate clients. If we had a motto, it would be Defuse the Threat. With a wry smile, I realize in this case, the threat is real, and it's my mother.

"You won't believe this," she says, leaning forward. "But the police don't have a crisis plan in place for the protests. They're still maintaining it'll be a peaceful gathering, and there won't be a need for crowd control." She whistles.

I sit back in my chair, and it creaks.

I say in a tight voice, "No need?"

She shakes her head. "Nope. We're on our own."

I pinch my lips and nod. "At least for now. I hope they'll wise up if things turn sour. If the police decide to use tear gas or pepper spray, do we have gas masks ready for the crew?"

"Yep." She points to a box by the door. "Right in there."

"Good. And the plastic zip ties?"

She indicates a second box. "In there."

"Let's hope those won't be necessary, and it'll be all kumbaya, singing along with guitar players, and listening to drum circles." I tap my chin. "I have to admit, I like the drumming. It's a catchy beat." I drum on the edge of the desk and grin. "Boom, diddly bop, boom, diddly bop, bap, bap, bap."

Mimi smiles. "It's early in the game, and you're already sounding punchy."

She may be right. If I am a bit off, I can blame it on my mother. Raising an index finger, I say, "And then the bongos come in, nice and high, picking up the beat and making it even better. Bop, diddly, bop, bop, bop."

Mimi cocks her head and looks concerned about me. "I agree, but it sounds like you might need to take a breather and get a break. Focusing on this event might be getting to you. And the fact that your mom is involved."

I grimace and fold my arms. If only Daisy wasn't meddling with Millersville. But wishing her away won't make it happen. I've got to find a way to be professional and ignore my mother's presence.

She says, "But I see what you mean. If we weren't working this job, I might go out there, and mix it up, and listen to the music. Some of those people with picket signs have good points."

"I agree," I say. "Like no more layoffs. A clean environment. No big brother controlling our decisions in the tech world. It does have appeal." I slap the arm of my chair. "But it's our job to make sure Mr. Brinker's company is secure. How are the security guards we hired doing over there? Any dustups so far?"

"They just reported in. The perimeter is secure. Trade delegates are slipping in through the back door unnoticed. Employees were told to leave the logo gear at home, and they're complying with that." She pauses. "We did have a group try to set up a sound stage in the back parking lot, but our team was able to move them off the premises by saying it was private property."

"Excellent, you're doing a fabulous job. If I ever leave the company, which I won't, I can see you stepping into my shoes and taking over. But that'll never happen. I love my job, and you guys are the best crew I've ever worked with."

She smiles. "Thanks, boss. The feeling is mutual."

I get up and motion to the door. "That's enough team love for the day, or I'll turn into a real softie. Get out of here, and keep up the good work. We'll get through this and come out the other side laughing at the Brown Lantern and toasting with a beer in our hands."

She pauses at the door. "By tomorrow afternoon, the party will be over."

I say, "I wonder what will be left of our town by then? Will we come through this intact?"

She knocks on wood. "I sure hope so."

I slump in my seat and let out a sigh. I can't let the fact that my mother is on the opposing side get to me. But it grates. Deep in my heart, I'm a little girl, wanting to be loved and accepted for who I am. Her being in town has thrown me into a snake pit of tangled emotions.

Turning to my phone, I type an update for our client.

I nod to myself. I can do this. I'll be fine. Somehow, I'll find a way to walk the sharp razor's edge between my childhood and adult lives.

I realize, as I sit up straight, that it's time to learn to

balance what's going on in my head with how I feel in my heart. Work and family don't have to be kept separate. Drumming my fingers on the desk, I know the next few days won't be easy for several reasons. I'm being rocketed out of my comfort zone.

14

I text Brinker with an update, and it goes out with a satisfying swoosh. A few minutes later, he texts me to say all is going smoothly in the trade association talks. No interlopers have slipped into the building or disrupted sessions.

Mimi knocks on my open door and stands in the doorway.

"I forgot to tell you something important. I inspected the conference room at Bettermed when they had a coffee break and while you were at your house. I found two listening devices under the table, and another two in lamp shades of the standing lamps by the side table."

I stand up and tap a pen on my desk. "So, the game is heating up. I didn't find any when I checked before. You think they were placed by someone in the cleaning crew?"

She shakes her head. "I spoke with the receptionist at

the front desk. She said the guy watering the plants spent an unusually long amount of time in there. Especially since there are only two plants that need watering in the room. And she didn't recognize him. She said he looked kind of furtive when he came out. Not only that, he put his watering can down by the front door and just walked out."

I raise an index finger and jab the air. "Now we know who we're up against. Good work. Cancel the plant service and tell the cleaning crew not to come until the trade talks end. We can't take any more risks."

Mimi says, "I already did that. We won't have any more instances of people infiltrating that way."

I rub my chin. "That was a smart move on their part, wasn't it? If I were on the other side, I'd have tried that too."

She folds her arms. "This group is turning out to be wiser than we originally thought. It's not just a bunch of people marching with signs. Placing someone on the plant detail was devious. This is turning out to be a bigger assignment than we thought."

"Much more than we thought," I say. "But we'll see who is the winner at the end of the meetings. This is our town, not theirs."

She grins, and her blue eyes sparkle. "We'll be the ones who'll come out ahead."

My phone rings, and it's Ned, a reporter I know from Seattle. She got that nickname from her family, because as a baby she looked like her Uncle Ned. I met her when my last employer was brought down on charges of violating regulations for clinical testing and patient enrollment. Ned is the one who broke the story, and worldwide news coverage followed. We bonded after surviving the crisis and bringing the head of the company I worked for to justice.

Unfortunately, that meant my team and I were out of work when the company shut down. I opened my own shop and hired my team. Nothing is easier than working with trusted team members you know well. I can predict when they'll take a breath, and I know they'll protect me. As I would for each of them.

"I've got to take this call," I say.

Mimi leaves and closes the door behind her.

When I answer, I say, "Have you heard what's going on in Millersville?"

Ned says, "I have, and I'm in town. Can you meet me and go over what's happening, give me an overview from a professional's viewpoint?"

"I can't. I have a client in the mix, and I have a vested interest. I can't disclose who the client is for confidentiality reasons."

She says, "Sounds like you're in charge of Bettermed's security, aren't you?"

I narrow my eyes. On the job, Ned is persistent and a pain in the butt. She lives to dig up dirt and get the scoop ahead of other news outlets.

"I can't comment," I say. "I sign non-disclosure agreements with clients. Nice try though."

"Let's meet for coffee. I just drove into town, and it took forever. I'm dying for a soy milk latte."

I wince, imagining the chalky taste. In my world, you drink your coffee black, and you grab sleep when you can. Although I do wander off the tracks with pizza, where I order a thin crust and add artichoke hearts and basil with chicken. My team groans when I bring in a thin crust pizza for dinner when we're working late. Vincent tells me, "If it's pizza, it's got to be deep dish with pepperoni." "No olives," Mimi says. "Or pineapple," Flora chimes in. Fortunately for me, the topic of pizza is the only source of disagreements in the Outrigger office.

I glance out the window while I'm on the phone.

The yellow buses are driving away. Crowds of people are milling around. The situation is combustible, with so many aimless bodies looking for a purpose.

I say, "I wish I could get together, but I've got some things to attend to. Let's connect next week after this blows over."

"Too bad," Ned says. "I was hoping to feature you in my story."

"Hmm, hold on, let me think about it for a sec."

If my company appeared in the news, it would be good publicity. I do need more clients. After the trade association meetings end, my team will be mostly twiddling their thumbs until I drum up more business.

"You know what?" I say, "Why don't you come over to the office in a few minutes? You can meet my staff. Bring your own latte, though. We only serve black drip coffee."

I give her the address and suite number, and we hang up.

I stack the papers on my desk and slide them into a drawer, so she won't be able to read upside down while we're talking. I put my laptop in sleep mode and stride to the bullpen.

"Guys, we've got a reporter from Seattle coming here in a few minutes."

Vincent says, "Is it Ned?"

I nod. "That's right."

"She's great," he says.

Flora says, "I admire how she pushes for the truth to come out."

Mimi smiles. "Can't wait to say hi to her again."

"Well, don't get too cozy with her," I say. "Whatever we say may appear in print, even if we think it's off the record. There are no guarantees with hungry reporters. So, shut down whatever you're working on for the moment, and be ready to meet her and say a few words about why you do the work you do. We could use the free publicity if she mentions Outrigger Services."

Vincent scratches his chin. "Let's see. Why did I pick this line of work? To put food on the table, pay for medical insurance, and to buy baby clothes?"

I clap him on the back. He works out so much, he's

solid as a rock. "That's it, bring the family angle into it, and talk up the human-interest side of the story."

"What'll we do while she's here?" Flora says. "We need to monitor social media and the surveillance cameras."

Flora needs a nudge in the right direction sometimes, so I say, "Tell you what, after you greet Ned, hang out for five minutes and then leave. Walk the perimeter of Brinker's company, relieve the guard monitoring the front or back doors, so they get a break. Walk the streets and report back to me in private, not in front of the reporter, about the situation at hand. I want to know what people on the street are saying, and any plans they're about to set in motion."

Flora grins. She loves stepping up and taking on more responsibility. That's what I need in someone on my staff.

With a gleam in her eyes, she says, "Got it."

"Clear your desks," I say. "Turn any documents over. I consider her a friend, but she's highly motivated and observant. Nothing gets past her sharp eyes."

15

———

A few minutes later, Ned knocks on the door. Her blond-streaked hair is windblown. Bags under her eyes indicate she hasn't had much sleep.

I go over, and she gives me a hug, because she's that kind of person, a hugger. I'm more of a handshake kind of person, but I'm adaptable. At least that's what my last performance review said at my previous employer.

The situation with my mother flashes through my mind. I'm trying my hardest to adapt to her being in my face, and in my home, and using a microphone to stir up a crowd. But the power battle going on right now between us is one of the highest personal mountains I've had to climb. I might as well be in the snow with crampons on, slogging my way up to Camp Muir on Mt. Rainier, the way I feel now.

"I couldn't get coffee," Ned says. "The lines were out

into the street and snaking down the block. I need a jolt of caffeine to get my arms around this story. Can you brew a cup for me?"

I say, "Sure, but first, let me introduce you to my team, then we'll grab coffee. Come and meet everyone."

My staff stand up. Their computer monitors, I'm relieved to see, are on screen-saver mode so Ned won't glean insights from staring at them. Trade secrets are best kept close to the vest. No need to tell everyone reading the news how we get the job done.

Ned meets my team members, and they treat her like she's a rock star.

"I read all of your articles," Flora says with a smile.

Ned grins. "Glad to hear it. I'm hoping to come up with a top of the fold article out of what's happening in Millersville. Have you heard anything about what the protesters are planning?"

I shoot them a look to keep quiet about what I heard from the anonymous source over the phone. And to put a lid on what my mother blabbed at the meeting at the Depot.

Mimi shrugs. "Not really. We're keeping an eye out though. We need to be ready at a moment's notice to respond and protect our client's best interests."

I flash her a smile. Job well done. I couldn't have put it any better and hope Mimi's soundbite appears in print. Free advertising is what we need.

Ned writes in her notebook as she talks with them.

She turns to Vincent and says, "And why are you drawn to this line of work? What brings you to Outrigger Services?"

Vincent beams. "I love the work and the team. We're highly trained specialists in our field, and the element of danger appeals to me. I like the investigative side of it. But most of all, it's about my new baby." He pulls out his phone and shows Ned a photo of a cherubic child with curly brown hair. "That's my son, Nathan." He grins.

I smile at him. There's nothing more handsome than a man who is proud of his kids. A stab of envy hits me. I doubt my father is showing any pictures of me around. It's been so long since we saw each other or talked.

Ned says, "That's good material, I like it." She fills a page in the notebook and flips it over. "Readers will eat that up."

"Okay, thanks everyone," I say. "Go out and cover your assignments. Ned and I will chat for twenty minutes. Then I need you back in the office."

As they file out, I brew a fresh pot of coffee. Since we're a start-up company, I'm keeping costs down, and we're drinking a Safeway blend. Nothing fancy here, not yet anyway. But someday, I'd like to upgrade the beverage choices in the company kitchen.

While the pot burbles, and coffee drips into a Mr. Coffee that's seen better days, I lean against the kitchen counter and cross my arms.

"So, tell me what you're hearing," I say. "Any idea what's going to happen?"

She smiles and shakes a finger at me. "Oh no, you don't. I'm the one gathering information for an article. I'll ask the questions."

I grin. "You and I are in the business of gathering information. I call it intel, but you call it news. And we both rely on sources."

The coffeemaker beeps. I fill two mugs, hand her one, and pull a carton of milk from the frig.

"It's not soy, but it'll do," she says, pouring milk into her coffee.

"Let's head to my office."

I carry a cup of hot black coffee and set it down on my desk.

Ned takes a seat opposite me, and we skip the small talk.

She takes out her notebook and puts her phone on my desk. "Okay if I record this conversation?"

With a shrug, I hope I'll say the right things to bring in new business. What if I blow it and put my foot in my mouth? "Sure."

She taps her phone to set it to record. "How many people would you say are in town for the protests?"

I'm about to answer when the sound of glass shattering down on the street brings me to my feet. Ned joins me at the window, and we crane our necks.

Five people in black clothing wearing face masks are running down the street. They're carrying baseball bats. They stop and smash a storefront window with a bat.

I flinch and grip the window sill. The situation has changed at this moment from a peaceful protest to violence and criminal acts. The battle has begun.

Pulling out my phone, I dial 911 and report a crime in progress.

The dispatcher takes my name and says they'll send an officer to the scene.

The runners in black stop mid-block to stare at a shiny, new-looking blue BMW.

I open the window to hear better, and a cool breeze blows in, smelling of rain.

"Shit's getting real," Ned says next to me.

I nod. "Sure is. This is a turning point in what was supposed to be a peaceful protest."

She scribbles that down in her notebook.

"We are anarchists," one yells, smashing the car's side window with a bat.

Goose bumps prick my flesh. The job of taking care of my client just got harder with these clowns in town. This small band of fanatics is carrying out a reckless act.

"Rich people suck," a man yells as he batters the hood of the car with a bat.

People in jeans and sweatshirts gather around the car, yelling encouragement. Two guys in black jump on the roof and the hood of the car. The car is beyond dented by now.

"Get off," a man calls to the others on the car.

When the hood and roof jumpers land on the pavement, the man wields a bat and smashes the windshield until the glass cracks. Spider web circles appear where the bat lands blows. When he batters the glass again, the windshield falls in on itself.

He yells, "Turn the car over."

As one, the crowd surges and flips the car on its top in the street.

I squint to be sure what I'm seeing is real. It didn't take long for a peaceful march to erupt like this. But down below in the street, there's someone I know.

My mother is dusting her hands off on her caftan. She must have been one of the ones to overturn the car. Ralph, the tall leader with a long brown beard, stands near her with his fists held high in the air.

"Victory," Ralph yells. "We showed them."

He glances up and locks eyes with me. He points and cackles, elbowing my mother.

My mom nods, but a flicker of concern crosses her face as she stares at me. It almost looks as if she felt ashamed for a flash of a second. Or wished she was up here having coffee with me instead of rabble rousing.

When I was growing up, she'd come back from a protest at our state capitol and flop into an easy chair, exhausted. She'd say, "Get me a glass of water and a cup of coffee, will you? I'm exhausted. Standing in a picket line for hours is too much for my poor feet."

Now, Ned nudges me and points to the street with her pen. "Who's that? Do you know those people?"

I take a slow breath and consider what to say. If I don't tell her the truth, I suspect Ned will find out anyway. "That's Ralph, one of the leaders."

"And the woman next to him in the caftan? Who is she? She looked like she knew you just now."

With a sigh, I say, "She does. That's my mother. Her name is Daisy."

Ned's jaw hangs open. "You and your mother are on opposite sides of the protest?"

I clear my throat, wishing it wasn't true. "Yes."

"Now that's a story. My editor will love this angle. We'll focus on the family feud over both sides of the protest."

As a chill creeps up my spine, I imagine our family friction brought out in public for anyone to read. Angry posts online are sure to follow. If I were to predict which way the wind would blow, I'd say the general population would end up siding with my dear mother. She can talk a sweet game, and she knows how to make people like her. She'd gush about protecting the earth, and of course people would rally behind that, compared to a daughter who is in the business of protecting big companies.

Down below, a line of RVs and older motorhomes chug up the street and stop, blocking the way.

Someone pours gasoline on the flipped over BMW and lights it on fire. Flames rise. Crackling sounds fill the air. Smoke wafts over, making me cough.

Daisy runs over, waving her hands. "Don't burn the car."

A man in black clothes shoves her away and screams, "Stand back."

The crowd shuffles back, giving the burning car a wide berth.

With a boom, the car explodes, Flames shoot out. People scream and run back.

As the fire subsides, people gather around, singing and dancing. A line of drummers file past. The office window glass vibrates with the beat. Protesters mill around in tortoise and porpoise costumes, holding up signs.

The BMW gives off a stinking smell of burning plastic and rubber. It permeates my office, and I wrinkle my nose.

I slam the window shut, and the glass buzzes. I've seen enough. My team needs me to work on coordinating our response. We can't let this get ahead of us, or we'll be trying to corral chaos instead of controlling variables and creating a secure environment.

The firefighters haven't shown up, probably because the street is blocked, and they can't get through. Containment has taken on a whole new meaning and is my biggest concern. I hope the police are on top of this, but I don't see a cop in sight.

My phone buzzes with a text.

Mimi reports in. "Police officers in riot gear are coming down Commercial, heading toward the protesters."

My muscles tense. This has become dangerous. A

flash of worry crosses my mind, and I wonder if my mother will get caught in the clash with the cops.

I turn to Ned. "I'll see you out. I've got to get back to work."

She looks up from her phone and nods. "Understood. I've got to get out there and interview people."

She points out the window. "I hear the TV trucks can't get close to the action. I'd better get out there and interview people and get the story to my editor."

At the door, I say, "Be careful out there. Police are headed this way."

She smiles. "Don't worry. I live for this. I was born to report on evolving situations and crises."

16

I send a text to my team. "The reporter left. Come back to the office when you can."

I glance out the window, where the crowd is growing. My mom shouts through a megaphone. People chant back. Their voices are getting louder. The window glass hums, as if rattled by the recent change in our normally placid small town.

Vincent slides into his seat. He taps on his keyboard, and two computer screens come to life. He's monitoring chatter on social media, checking the news, and video feeds from our security cameras.

I go out to greet him. "What's going on out there?"

He blows out a breath. "It's heating up. Protesters are gearing up for a fight."

My jaw tenses. "My mother is out there. But don't treat her any different because of my relationship to her."

His eyes grow wide, and he sits back. "Your mother is involved in this? Did you know about that before we took the job?"

I groan. "No, I didn't. She mentioned she was taking a trip, and she wouldn't say where she was going. I had no idea."

As a headache throbs, I rub my temples. "Look out my office window, and I'll point her out."

He jumps to his feet, and we stand side by side, peering out.

I point to my mom, who is yelling. "That's her, with the megaphone."

He turns and stares at me. "That's your mother? You don't look anything alike."

With a shrug, I say, "My dad had a baby with my biological mom, who took off, and then my parents got together. Daisy raised me, but our natures are nothing alike."

He nods and rubs his chin. "I guess so."

"I think I inherited the law-abiding part of my personality from my father. Daisy's urge to make a better world by protesting didn't carry over to me, despite living in close proximity."

"Wow," he says, staring outside. "You sure you don't want her to receive special treatment if she makes a scene at Bettermed?"

I press my lips together. "Nope, treat Daisy like anyone else on the opposing side. If she comes near Brinker's company, and I heard they're planning a press conference outside his building tomorrow morning, we need to protect our client, no matter what."

"Understood." He goes back to his desk.

My fingers drum on the windowsill. My curiosity urges me to leave the office and watch what my mom is up to first-hand. I want to monitor the street activity with my own eyes.

I pocket my phone and say to Vincent, "I'm leaving you in charge. I'll be on my cell if you need me."

Taking the stairwell down from the second floor, I barge out of the exit door and look around.

The air is cool. A swift breeze is kicking up food wrappers left on the ground. Our town typically doesn't have litter. We take pride in being a tidy town.

Eyeing up a burger wrapper, I roll my eyes. Save the planet but trash the town where you're protesting. That seems to be the motto of the crowd.

I stroll past a few stragglers leaning against a brick wall in the alley. Hands in my pockets, I stare at the pavement and eavesdrop, hoping to hear hints of what's coming up.

A woman in her twenties in a blue plaid flannel shirt and purple shoulder-length hair says, "I don't get why we have to get up so early tomorrow. I always sleep until noon."

I slow my pace to listen and pick up a soda can. I'll

look like I'm cleaning the street with good intentions, but really, I'm spying on them.

A young man pushes back his long brown hair. "Ralph said we need to be there to show solidarity outside the trade meeting location. He said the press conference is going to make us famous and get publicity for the movement. It'll be shown all over the world."

I move on before they can ask what I'm doing. A swarm of people block my way on Commercial, but I shoulder through and toss the can in a trash receptacle. Tomorrow morning at Brinker's company will be a show down. If I manage it right, it'll blow over and dash the opposing side's hopes and expectations for a meaningful news event.

Ten drummers march down the street heading north. Boom da boom, bap, bap, bap, the drum beats thrum. More drummers follow behind the first group. The pavement transmits the rhythm to my feet.

Someone slams into my shoulder as they push past, following the parade.

A young woman in a blue ball cap turns and says, "Sorry about that."

It's Ned. I lift my hand to acknowledge her and hope she won't get crushed in the crowd. She moves on.

Stepping aside, I lean against a building where office products are sold. A mattress is on display in the store front window. I tilt my head. Office products and mattresses is an odd combination. Or is it a statement about people working so much that they need to sleep at the office, like I'm doing this week?

People dressed as turtles and dolphins go by holding signs emblazoned with slogans. "Clean up the oceans' garbage patch." "Stop polluting." "Protect sea creatures."

Next comes my mother in a yellow caftan. She's shaking a tambourine, which is her favorite instrument, and using a megaphone. She keeps her eyes trained ahead and doesn't glance my way.

"Stick together, and stay united," she calls. "They can't keep us down."

A sea of people marches past with thundering feet, repeating my mom's words.

I nod. That's my mom, and I guess I'm proud of her standing up for her beliefs. But did you have to do it here, on my watch, and against my client, and in my town? I'm about to slip away to check on Brinker's company when the parade halts.

People in back bump into those in front.

Whistles blow.

A woman screams. People shout. I can't see my mom, but I hear her voice.

She yells, "Stand back. We have a right to protest. We have a permit."

Protesters turn and run, scattering like leaves in the wind.

Police officers in blue advance down Commercial. They're carrying plastic shields in front of their bodies and wielding clubs. There are only ten of them. Stark fear is etched across their faces.

I hurry up steps to the post office. From this vantage point, I'm out of the way and closer to my client's building, which is two blocks down. I cross my fingers and make a wish for Daisy to come out of this fracas unharmed.

17

———

The police officers march down the street. Just then, an older woman in her seventies with gray hair in a fresh perm exits Tangles Hair Salon across from the Post Office, where I'm standing. She fumbles in her purse, looking for something as she walks on the sidewalk.

A stout police officer says in a booming voice, "Clear the street."

The older woman continues along her way. Her skirt sways as she walks.

Without warning, the officer holds up a can and sprays her with a substance.

She claps her hands over her eyes and shrieks. "I can't see. My eyes are burning."

The beauty shop door flies open. A woman in her

forties rushes out and ushers the gray-haired woman inside. The beautician locks the door and pulls down the blinds. This is not a day for normal business operations.

I text my team. "Police are using pepper spray on civilians. Be careful out there."

An officer yells, "Disperse, or we'll arrest you."

Daisy hops up on a bench by the curb.

She raises her fist and yells through the megaphone, "We have rights. We can protest if we want."

A police officer walks up and pepper sprays her. It drifts through the air, and makes my eyes smart. My mom yelps and swings the megaphone, but the officer is already moving down the street.

I blink back tears and breathe a sigh of relief when Ralph appears and puts a bottle of water in Daisy's hands. She tilts her head back and pours water over her face.

I bite my lower lip. Daisy is my mom, not a stranger at a rally, and I'm worried about her welfare. Although I wish she wasn't stirring up trouble in my town, I understand the need to follow your passion. Mine is to protect people. Daisy's is to protect the environment and defend our rights, among her causes.

When she wipes her eyes and looks around, we nod to each other. I put a hand to my heart and hold it up to her. I mouth the words, "Be careful."

She returns the gesture, and I slip away, heading toward Bettermed where the STA trade talks are being held. Staying close to buildings and away from roaming police officers, I hurry down the sidewalk.

An older recreational vehicle that blocked a side street is being towed away.

A County transit bus stops with a groan of the brakes. A second one comes behind, and a third follows. Their engines are running and emitting fumes that cloud the air. I cringe and wonder if those buses are bringing more protesters to the party. If so, I doubt ten police officers can handle the growing skirmish.

No wonder the cops looked scared. I wouldn't want to be one of them. The odds of ten prevailing against thousands aren't even in the realm of possibility. But then again, the police could have ordered the buses to be positioned there to take protesters to jail.

Across the street from the Bettermed building, a folk singer on a stage strums a guitar and sings a protest song. A sound system amplifies his voice, and it bounces off stone walls and echoes. It sounds like a hundred million singers are throwing their voices into the protest.

Gathered around the stage, five hundred or more people clap their hands and sing along. A toddler in overalls sits on the shoulders of a thirty-something year old man in a tie dye shirt. People wave their arms in a happy gathering, but given the pepper spray that's coming, I'd say the tone of the event is about to change.

I sniff the damp air. We've had a break in the rain, and

the showers let up. But I have a feeling we're in for a deluge of a storm.

The singer strums on stage, and the crowd claps in time, swaying to the music.

The atmosphere is cheerful and collegial, until a police officer announces, "Leave now, or you'll be arrested. Buses are waiting to transport you to jail."

The county transit buses chug up the side street and stop. The doors open.

The folk singer says, and the microphone carries his words to everyone for a block around, "No way. We won't go. You can't make us."

The crowd cheers. Hands raised, they chant, repeating the singer's words.

Heavy footsteps come down the street. Police are lined up side by side, five deep. They must've gotten reinforcements from afar. Finally, it looks like the police chief is aware of the reality on the ground. The optics of his being out of town at the beginning of the mess aren't going to go over well with taxpayers.

Officers handcuff protesters and lead them to the first waiting bus.

The protesters are singing as they file onboard with hands behind their backs.

When a woman falls to the ground and lies prone, kicking her legs, she's dragged off by two officers, shoving their hands under her armpits.

A man shouts and resists arrest. He crosses his arms and remains rigid, but he's shoved onto a bus. He yells, "Police brutality."

The group doesn't pick up his protest or repeat it, and he looks forlorn, leaning against a window.

Television newscasters speak on camera and gesture to the dispersing crowd. A reporter looks like she just came from a beauty salon, and it wasn't one that served pepper spray on the side. Her auburn hair has soft bangs and flows over her shoulders. She's well-groomed and armed for a media appearance.

I run my fingers through my hair. I'd rather work behind the scenes, orchestrating with my team, than make a public appearance. If we do our job right, no one will notice us. We're the stagehands at the Ballet, pulling ropes so the sets change behind closed curtains.

A bus closes the door and starts up, taking a left and going toward the Port Shed to avoid the crowds on Commercial. Soon, a second bus loaded with passengers departs with handcuffed passengers, and a third pulls up.

My phone dings with an incoming text.

Mimi says, "I'm back at the office. The police chief announced a curfew tonight of ten pm."

I nod. "I'm glad to know he's finally doing something about the situation."

After checking in with my staff outside the building entrances, I go in to chat with Brinker. His assistant says he's in the trade talks, so I text him. "Can you meet in the lobby for a few minutes? Situation is escalating. I've got an update."

He walks out of the conference room a few minutes later. His cheeks are flushed. His pristine silver hair is out of place. Activities in town had gotten to us. We'll never be the same.

I raise an eyebrow, thinking of my mother. Daisy and I will have a changed relationship, for sure, after the Millersville protests come to a close. I'm not entirely sure we'll be on speaking terms after she betrayed me in public and broke into my home.

I say, "Thanks for stepping away for a quick word."

His smile looks strained. "I was glad for an excuse. We've got a member making his point for far too long. We need to move to a vote and not yammer on."

I say in a low voice, "The police are using pepper spray on protesters and passersby. They handcuffed people and are taking them to jail in buses. A car was overturned and burned. It's dangerous out there. There's a curfew in place for tonight at ten o'clock."

Brinker frowns.

I say, "I recommend you close the trade talks now, before things get worse. Protesters will be here tomorrow morning to hold a press conference out front. But before the curfew tonight, I'll prepare the building and have it ready to thwart the protesters' press conference plans."

He nods. "I agree with you. We'll vote on the issues

and close the meeting early. I don't want attendees hurt while going back to their hotels or cars. I'll have them leave by the back entrance and do their best to blend in."

Belinda from the trade association comes over to us. She glances at me, and her eyebrows furrow. "We're ready for you, Mr. Brinker, in the conference room."

He hurries away.

She stays behind for a beat and says in a sing-song voice, "Too bad you didn't make it for the afternoon refreshments. You look windblown and like you could use a rest. And maybe a makeover."

I cross my arms and give her the stink eye. She strikes me as someone who is more worried about her appearance than contributing to a cause. I'm committed to authenticity and achieving a greater goal, and I hammer that message into my team every morning after I run. "Get it done, and be your best. We can do this."

My guys raise their water bottles, or coffee mugs, or clenched fists and say, "Yes, today will be our best day yet."

Now, I say to the trade association coordinator, "My focus is on containing the threat to the discussions here." It occurs to me that my mother is part of the threat outside, but I keep that to myself. I add, "Results matter more than how I look."

Just then, a broad-shouldered man barges into the lobby. He must've gotten past the security guard we posted at the front entrance.

He holds up a sign and says, "No more layoffs. Protect the workers. Get the billionaires off our backs."

Belinda arches an eyebrow and leans in, saying to me in a low voice, "Hope you can handle that. Good luck."

She sashays away, leaving me to deal with the intruder.

18

———

I'm wearing a headset that I haven't had to use yet, and I speak into it. "Perimeter breach. A protester is in the client's lobby. Get here fast, if you can."

I turn to the invader and size him up. He's medium height and weight and has a first-class angry snarl on his face. His face is flushed, and his blue eyes are glazed. I wonder if he's had too much to drink or if he's on drugs. Or he could be flushed with the fervor that fills my mother and wanting to prove he's a leader in the movement.

I gesture to the registration counter. "I'd like to talk to you over there for a moment. It won't take long. I want to hear your views. Maybe I can learn something from you."

He cocks his head, looking confused, as if he expected to be tossed out. With a shrug, he walks over. We lean against the counter like old friends.

"Tell me what's upsetting you," I say, hoping my reinforcements will arrive soon. "Did you get laid off? Because I did last month, and it was really tough on me and my whole team."

He rubs his cheek. "I did, and I can't get work. I can't find a job that pays near as much as Hefty Software paid me in Seattle. I'm having trouble paying the mortgage, and my husband and I just bought the place last year." He wipes a tear from his eyes.

"Oh, man," I say, nodding and doing my best to sound understanding, kind and compassionate. Because no one deserves to be laid off and left in the cold without a way to pay the bills. It's worse than falling into the ice-cold Salish Sea water in winter.

"That sounds like an impossible situation," I say. "I hear you, and I can see why you're protesting and railing against the system."

He sets down his sign and lets out a heavy sigh. "I just want to stay in my house, take care of my loved ones and live the good life. Is that too much to demand?"

"No, it isn't."

Mimi hustles through the front door and heads toward me for strength in numbers.

I nod to her and hold up a finger to hold back and wait.

I say to the man, "What's your name? I'm Violet."

"Chris," he says, scuffing a foot. "Am I going to be

arrested for coming in and pushing past the guard at the entrance?"

"I don't think so. As long as you don't keep yelling and leave peacefully, I think we can let it go." I gesture to Mimi to join us, and she comes over.

"Chris here is upset. He lost his software job in Seattle and is having financial troubles. Do you think we should turn him over to the police? Or send him on his way?"

Mimi says to Chris, "Hey, I know how you're feeling. We lost our jobs when the company we worked for crashed. It's scary, and you feel out of control. You want to take it out on someone, but that won't do any good."

Tears trickle down Chris' cheeks. "I just want it all back. The life I had. Working from home four days a week. Making a difference on a team. Now I'm stuck applying online for jobs that are way beneath my skill level. And if I hear anything back, they tell me I'm over-qualified. The situation is unbearable." He blows his nose on a tissue and honks like a Canada goose.

The employee at Bettermed who is staffing the reception counter comes over and says, "I couldn't help but overhear your story. We're hiring here. We don't do remote work, so you'd have to move to Millersville. You can look online for open positions and mention my name. I'm Lucinda Hollinger."

Chris shakes her hand. "Thanks, I'll talk with my husband about the idea and see what positions you have open. We've always liked this area. The valley is so pretty in the spring when the tulips are in bloom." He smiles.

Mimi and I make eye contact and nod to each other. The situation has been defused.

Chris goes to the door, leaving his protest sign on the floor.

I pick it up and take it to him. "You forgot your sign. Here you go."

He waves it away. "No thanks. I'm going home to talk to Derek about moving somewhere like here so I can find work. Seattle's changed anyway, and the crime is getting to us. Syringes in the parks and on the beaches. Cars broken into."

I cock my head. "It's not nirvana here either. Our crime rate is increasing. Cars are getting broken into. I wouldn't want you to think we're touting a perfect town and have you be disappointed."

"Nowhere is perfect," he says. "Family is what matters most. And friends too, of course."

A flicker of sadness hits me when he mentions family. I say, "Good luck. Maybe we'll see you around."

I close the exterior door and stick his protest sign behind the counter. Someone else can deal with it later. Or, who knows, maybe one of Brinker's employees might spot it and take the sign out for a spin on Commercial among the masses.

The conference room doors bang open. Women and

men stream out. They're in a hurry and heading with purpose for the back exit.

I call out, "Don't call attention to yourselves out there. Blend in and get out of town as fast as you can. There's a curfew in place for tonight, but I doubt people will stick to it."

Brinker comes over to me and wipes his forehead with a handkerchief. "Glad that's over. It'll be easy from now on, won't it?"

I shake my head. "I'm afraid not, sir. I was just outside and despite the police hauling protesters off to jail, there are still thousands of people on the streets. The arrests agitated the leaders. My recommendation is to close the company early. Send your employees home and give them the day off tomorrow."

His head jerks back, and his eyes open wide. "You're talking about hours of lost productivity. I can't do that. We have deadlines to meet."

"Understood. How about asking them to work from home the rest of today and tomorrow? Or using some of those wellness days you talked about? I don't want anyone to get hurt, and we can't predict how the mob will react. The police are using pepper spray, and that's likely riled up the protesters even more."

He scratches his chin.

I say, "I saw one of the leaders get pepper sprayed out there by a police officer. She was spitting mad." I decide to divulge more about my personal relationship for transparency. "I happen to know her."

"You do? How's that possible?"

"Well, sir, to be honest, she's my mother. And I can tell you when she gets crossed and thinks an injustice has occurred, she'll go to the ends of earth to hunt the perpetrator down and prove her point. You don't want to hear about the contractor who stiffed her on fixing the roof after my dad moved out."

He whistles. "That's very interesting. So, this could get worse. It's hard to imagine, but I'll take your word for it. You'll be here tomorrow morning before they hold the press conference outside?"

I nod. "I will, you can bet on it. And if you need my company's help tonight, a few of us will be sleeping at the office, so we're right down the street. Just call or text, and we'll be here in a few minutes." I cross my arms and grin with pride. "We're known for our fast response times. We run to trouble."

He smiles. "Good to know. I sure am glad I hired your company. But you say your mother is out there on the opposite side? That's just too strange, isn't it?"

I purse my lips. "To say it's frustrating is an understatement. It is unfortunate. I suppose it gives us an advantage though, because we can predict what Daisy might do before she acts and convinces others to follow her lead."

He thrusts a finger in my direction. "But the same is

true on the opposite side. She knows you and will be second-guessing your next move."

I hold up my hands. "You're right. We'll see what tonight and tomorrow will bring. I'm looking forward to being done with these protests. Finished, done, and dusted, and the danger will be banished."

"I couldn't agree with you more," he says. "I'll see you tomorrow."

We say goodbye, and he leaves for his office.

I make my way to the door. I'm looking forward to taking my team out for beers tomorrow evening when everything settles down in town. And going back to my bed at home. Which reminds me, I need to make sure someone on my staff drives past my house and checks to be sure my mom and her friends haven't broken in again.

Outside the Bettermed building, the stage is empty. A few people are milling around or standing in groups of two or three. The police action of taking people to jail has temporarily quieted this part of town.

I walk to the office and watch workers in coveralls set barricades in place along a block of Commercial.

A man wipes his brow and says to a co-worker, "That's all we've got."

"We don't have more?" a grizzled fellow says. "This won't do much."

The first man shrugs. "The police chief didn't expect this many people. Not enough warning."

I grit my teeth and continue to the office. Up ahead,

several hundred people are standing in the street, listening to a speaker who is standing on a bench.

I grit my teeth. Daisy is leading the cause. I listen and nod, admiring her passion and purpose. She isn't holding back. We're different but alike in that way.

19

When the crowd quiets in the late afternoon and disperses for a spell, I head over to my client's building to prepare for our Operation Surprise that will be revealed tomorrow morning. A local contractor shows up at the front entrance with a crew and a lift.

He scratches his chin. "It was tough to get through the side streets just now. It's quite a commotion in town, isn't it?"

"Sure is," I say, hoping all will go well and no one will get hurt. We just need to get through tonight and tomorrow, and then it should be all over. My feet throb, and my throat is parched. I could use a rest.

I'd like to sit in the office with a cold beverage and put my feet up on the desk and play Wordle on my phone, but

I can't take a break until this party ends. Tomorrow afternoon, I keep telling myself. Just hang in there until then. You've been through much worse. You can make it.

"Okay," I say, "let's get started. First of all, I need you and your men to keep this to yourselves. We won't pay you if you or your guys talk about what we're about to do."

His bushy eyebrows shoot up. "Top secret? Fine. I just do the work. Nothing to yammer on about at the tavern or at home with the wife and kids."

I nod. "Excellent. We got that out of the way." Pointing, I say, "I'd like you to take down the company sign right there at the entrance. You said you had a warehouse to store it in for a few days?"

"I do. All right, we'll haul away the sign."

"And bring it back in two days."

He pulls off his blue ball cap. "And what else?"

"Paint over where the sign was, so it looks like the walls have always been bare. Did you bring the paint like I asked you to?"

"Sure thing." He moves his chin, indicating the back of his truck. "It's in with the painting gear. We're careful, and we won't leave a mess behind. So, you'll hire us again next time." He grins, and his blue eyes sparkle.

I gesture to the front entrance wall. "Great, I'll leave you to it. I'll be right over here on the bench if any questions come up. A curfew is in place, it starts at ten. I hope you can get out of here by then?"

"No problem." He turns to his two workers, who are also wearing white coveralls. "Let's get moving and get 'er done."

I stay busy on my phone checking news feeds and texting with my team while they work. The lift whines, as if carrying away the company logo sign is too big a burden. This whole operation of protecting my client has been a chore. But not one I'd shy away from if I'd known all the facts ahead of time.

They wrap up several hours later, and I pull a wad of money out of my pocket. Over the phone when I hired him, I promised to pay in cash for the job, since it was short notice, and they'd be working late. I figured he and his crew needed an extra incentive to make their way through the clogged streets and show up.

I peel off a bunch of fifty-dollar bills and hand them over. "That's half the amount we talked about. I'll pay you the rest when the sign is back up."

He nods and stuffs the money in his pocket. He extends a warm hand, and we shake. He's got a firm grip, which makes me respect him all the more. He's prompt, and he delivered on his promise.

He says, "We'll be back in two days, like you asked, and put it all back."

"Thanks so much. I appreciate you showing up on short notice. I'll pay you the rest when the sign's back up."

He and his two helpers wipe their hands on their

white coveralls and hop in the truck, driving off in growing darkness.

Footsteps approach, coming closer, from many people.

People shout.

Two people in black clothing and face masks run toward me.

My body stiffens. What are they planning? How many of them are there?

I contact my team using the headset. "Protesters are on the move near Bettermed. I think something is about to happen. Stand by."

I move closer to the action, making my way down Commercial. I keep to the side of the street, moving past storefronts.

Anarchists dressed in black with full black face masks over their heads yell.

I step into a darkened doorway, out of the street light's glare. It's not my job to quell this angry mob. That's why we have a police department. But I don't see a cop in sight. Just two abandoned barricades. A lot of good those will do without officers behind them to corral insurgents.

An anarchist lifts a baseball bat and smashes a window. Glass shatters. I cringe at the sound of exploding glass.

A woman's screams pierce the air.

"Go away," she says. "This is my shop. I'll protect it until I die."

She pulls out a stun gun. "I'll zap you if I have to."

The leader in black says to the others, "Come on, let's get out of here."

The gang of about twenty people in black runs down the street heading south.

The store keeper slumps to her doorstep and weeps, putting her head in her hands.

From a doorway, I update my team. "Anarchists are on the move, heading north. Tell the police. I'm across from the post office where they broke windows in a shop."

"Roger that," Mimi says. "We're on it."

Before I hurry away, I stop to console the shop owner. "That's tough, what just happened to you. I saw it take place, and it's being reported to the police right now."

She looks up with watery eyes and sniffs. "Where are the cops when you need them? I shouldn't have to be here, defending my store. They should be patrolling."

She holds up her hands and wails. "How am I going to deal with this? The plate glass is missing. Anyone could get in and take my inventory. I've got all my money invested in this store. I can't afford to replace them or make repairs."

She bursts into a fresh round of tears.

A pair of orange running shoes catches my eye.

"Hey," I say, "I like those shoes. I'll come back in two days and buy a pair. If you don't have my size, I'll order them. I'll tell my co-workers and friends. We're all into nice running shoes. Can't have enough. Always gotta have a back-up pair in the closet."

She rubs her eyes. "What size are you?"

"Nine."

"We'll have to order them. I'm not sure how long it'll take."

"Don't worry about it," I say. "I'll wait however long it takes. We're all in this together in town. This shouldn't have happened to you."

She clenches her fists. "Those darn hoodlums. They're making a mess out of what was billed as a peaceful protest. I thought I might sell some shoes, but instead no one is coming in. The parade marches by, and no one stops." She whimpers. "I've had it up to here with slow business. This is the last straw."

"Man, that's rough," I say. "Listen, do you need someone to board up your window tonight? Would it be all right if I made a call and see if I can find someone to do that?"

She frowns. "It's late, and there's a curfew in place. No one will want to come down here with that going on." She points down the street in the direction the vandals took off.

I hold up a finger. "At least let me try."

"Okay, thanks," she says, getting up from her stoop.

I dial the contractor, who picks up right away. It sounds like he's in a bar, with booming music in the background.

"This is Violet. Do you have a minute?"

He says, "Did we miss something?"

"Not at all. But the anarchists just broke windows along Commercial and are heading south on foot. Might you have time to help a distressed store owner? Her window was smashed, and she's got a load of expensive shoes here, exposed to anyone walking by. I know it's a big ask, but you'd really be helping her out if you brought over two sheets of plywood and secured her store before the anarchists come back."

I bite my lip and hope he'll say yes.

The store owner says, "I can pay him something, but not much."

He speaks with someone in the background and says into the phone. "My guys and I will run over to Home Depot, get the plywood and come back. Where are you?"

"Oh, that's wonderful. It's across from the post office. You can't miss it. The owner will be here."

"My name is Freddie," she says. "I'll be waiting. Tell him thank you a million zillion times."

"Her name is Freddie, and she'll be here waiting," I tell him. "Thanks for being one of the good guys. I have to leave and take care of some things."

He chuckles. "You're on a secret mission?"

I smile. "You might say that. But I can't talk about it or even acknowledge what you said. Bye, now."

I hang up and say, "He'll be here in a while. He has to

drive to the valley and get plywood. Will you be okay here on your own?"

She holds up her stun gun. "I'm armed and ready. You go on ahead. And thanks so much."

"You bet. But don't be trigger happy with that. You could really hurt someone."

My staff fills me in at the office while I lean against a wall chugging a bottle of water. Posts on social media indicate protesters expect tomorrow to be the big day, the one they've been building up to. The crescendo.

Mimi checks her notes and says, "The protesters are saying online that this town hasn't seen anything yet. Tomorrow, they're going to blast their point across in a battle for control of the streets and confront the issues at hand."

I shove my hands in my pockets. "It's a good thing the trade delegates left. They all slipped out of town unnoticed."

Vincent holds up a hand. "Except one. She called and asked for help. She said she was in her rental van, but it was surrounded by the mob. Somehow, the protesters got wind that she was with the trade association and followed her to the vehicle. They started rocking it, and she was screaming, but a few of us ran over and with the help of two officers, we held the people off so she could drive away." He shakes his head. "She was bat-shit mad, said she'd never come back to this freaking town ever again."

I say, "Was her name Belinda?"

He nods. "Yep."

I make a face. She's the one who said I needed a makeover. But I wouldn't wish the worst on anyone. She must've been frightened down to her painted toenails to see the crowd surrounding her van. All that shouting from a mob must have made her knees tremble with fear.

"Good work, guys. And I suppose it's my fault. We should've arranged for them to be escorted to their cars or have transport out of town."

Mimi says, "I did see on the Facebook page for the event that a group of trade meeting delegates got into a stretch limo. They were seen scurrying into it behind the post office. But the car took off before the protesters could get to it. People tried to stop the car and pull people out to teach them a lesson. They wanted to make them take public transport or the shuttle to SeaTac Airport instead of a cushy ride that none of the 99 percent could afford."

Vincent presses his lips together. "The income gap and wealth disproportion issue is important to the folks coming here from across the country."

"And from around the world," Mimi says. "It's burning

them up with resentment, and they're here to make their voices heard."

I bite down on a fingernail. The wealth gap is a huge issue. I do my best to smooth out potential resentments in my company by paying my people well. I understand why protesters are ticked off about the massive difference in net worth between their households and the top dogs who were in town making decisions about software that will affect their lives.

I clear my throat. "They have a valid point, but the thing is, the protests have turned from a peaceful gathering to what could be considered a riot. The anarchists running down the streets smashing store windows are detracting from the main message."

Mimi says, "They're certainly getting media attention. All the national and local TV channels are talking about the gang in black marauding the streets, making it dangerous."

I nod. "And so far, the police aren't helping to calm the situation. I saw a little old lady today fresh out of the beauty shop who was pepper sprayed by a cop."

Vincent shakes his head. "That's an out of proportion response, and not what the cops should be doing. It just riled people up even more."

"They're afraid," I say. "You could see it on their faces."

Mimi leans against her desk. "Someone caught the police pepper spraying the little old lady in a video on their phone and sent it in to KING-5 news. They're showing it over and over. It makes the police look incompetent, or like they're out to hurt innocent bystanders. It's not good optics."

I sigh. "They're afraid. The chief blew it off, said it wouldn't be a big deal and not many people would come. They've been caught short, and they're understaffed for a mass protest. What are your contacts with the police and at city hall saying? Any plans for tomorrow?"

Mimi says, "Apparently they have additional barricades coming on a truck in the morning."

I lift an eyebrow. "Only on one truck? Is that all?"

She nods. "Yep, and they've put in an urgent order for more clubs and pepper spray and shields." She looks up. "I guess they used up their supply of pepper spray and ran out."

"Well, that might be a good thing, if they didn't run around spraying passersby. Are they gearing up for tomorrow? Taking new measures for crowd control?"

"My source wouldn't say any more about that. She got tight-lipped and shut down. She said she had to get off the phone and hung up right away."

I tap my lips. "Okay, so we know the situation will be building tomorrow, and there might even be panic in the streets if the police use unnecessary force. Our job is to protect our client's building and advise him on how to protect his employees. He sent them home, thank goodness, earlier this afternoon and told them not to come into work tomorrow. So that's one worry off our list of things to manage."

Vincent raises a hand. "About city hall, I hear the mayor is going crazy about all this. She's worried about the impact it'll have on tourism. Who wants to take a vacation to a small waterfront town and get mobbed by angry protesters? That's the look we have on the national news right now. Hotel and motel bookings are being cancelled. Whale watching boats say nobody's calling, like they usually do. The Chamber of Commerce and other groups are riding the mayor hard about sorting this out right now, before further damage occurs to their businesses and the town's reputation."

I say, "It's a shit storm, and we can't pretend it isn't. We're doing our best to contain it. There's no maraschino cherry to go on top of this acrimony sundae. I hope it doesn't put off new businesses coming here and setting up headquarters. I was hoping to sign on more local clients to minimize travel for us, so you could see your families more and be home at night."

A glance flickers between them, and I say, "I know it's tough, working this gig and staying on the job when your families are waiting for you right here in the area. Believe me, by tomorrow afternoon, I hope this will all be put to bed, Then you can run home to your loved ones, give them a hug and collapse on the couch. But before that happens, after this is over, I'd like to take you out for a beer to celebrate our success. We'll have protected our client through a protest that thundered in the streets."

Vincent's left eye twitches. That happens when he's worried about working long hours and is missing seeing his baby and wife.

The thought of family reminds me of how my mother broke into my place. My brows furrow. The latch on my back door is loose, and I've been meaning to replace it. What with starting my own company and hiring staff, I've been preoccupied.

I say to them, "How about you take the rest of the night off and go check on your families? Be back at six in the morning. But watch out, because the curfew is in place. Drive slowly."

He checks the time. "Thanks, but if I go home at this hour, I'll just wake everyone and get the baby excited. It'd be best if I just stayed here for the duration. I told my wife I'd be home tomorrow evening after we wrap up."

Mimi smiles. "I sent Flora out to gather intel, see if she can sniff anything out. But I'll take you up on the offer. Thanks, boss." She tucks her cell in a pocket. "See you tomorrow at the crack of dawn."

When she leaves, Vincent says, "What about you? What're you going to do?"

I check the time. It's eleven on the nose. I'm tired, but I'm also wired. Tomorrow afternoon can't come soon enough. It's our first assignment for this client, and my staff is kicking ass, taking names, and going above my expectations.

I say to Vincent, "I have to go by my house to make sure my mom and her friends aren't camped out or raiding the place."

"I'll go with you," he says. "You might need a second set of hands."

"I'd appreciate that. They're staying at the RV park, but they were whining about standing in line for the showers. If I know my mom at all, I suspect she and her friends may feel entitled to take advantage of the comforts of my home, even though I kicked them out and was clear about their not coming back."

I glance out a window into the dark night.

"But let's wait until Flora gets back."

21

———

Flora looks beat when she comes back to the office. She's got dark circles under her eyes from working long hours, and her hair lacks luster. If anyone was in need of a makeover, it's all of us at Outrigger Services.

Flora is breathing hard. She wipes a sheen of sweat from her brow and says, "The anarchists are running down Commercial busting windows. Protesters are following them and helping themselves. Police officers aren't around to stop the looting. And two people are spray painting buildings with messages like, Take control and Fight back."

I hand her a water bottle, and she opens it and drinks.

I say, "They need more than five cops on the force for something like this. They're understaffed and overwhelmed. I hope the Chief will call in reinforcements from other towns."

Vincent rubs his forehead. "I wouldn't want to be in their shoes facing angry activists."

My phone rings, and it's my neighbor, Marvin, from across the street.

I answer it and say, "Hello?"

His voice is hoarse, as if he's been yelling, "I called the police about a disturbance at your place. But they said they're too busy to deal with it now."

My pulse quickens, and I grip the phone tight. My body breaks out in a sweat.

In a tight voice, I say, "What's going on at my house?"

"People are dancing around a bonfire in your yard. I went over and told them to leave. But one woman said she was your mother, and she had permission. Is that right? Did you invite them to be there and raise hell while you're away?"

I smack my forehead. Vincent and Flora watch me with wide eyes. My mom is making a tough week much worse. When I was young, she was often in the sunroom sitting on the floor, meditating with crystals close at hand. I made my own peanut butter sandwiches. Sure, I made a mess, but I tried to clean it up. I had to eat.

Blowing out a breath, I say, "My mother does not have permission to be there. I told her and her friends to leave yesterday. I'll be over right away."

"Bring help, because there's a lot of them."

I hang up and turn to Flora and Vincent. "There's a group camped out at my house, and we need to send them away. The police weren't able to respond to my neighbor's call."

Vincent says, "And your mother is there?"

I sigh. "Yes, she is, and I wish she wasn't anywhere near this town. I didn't need to deal with this, not this week and not tonight."

The three of us pile into my car. As I drive, I keep an eye out for patrol cars, given that we're violating the curfew. There's no police presence. Away from downtown, the streets are quiet.

I roll the window down for fresh air and take a deep breath of briny sea air coming off Cedar Channel. The smell normally calms me, but there's no hope of that now. Not when I'm about to confront my mother, Daisy, the threat.

Gripping the steering wheel tight, I realize I'm more nervous about this encounter than others during my career. Somehow putting my mom in the mix makes it all the more frightening. Not only professional, but personal stakes are involved.

I say, "Let's make a plan before we get there."

Vincent says, "Are you thinking you'll deal with your mother? Or should we?"

Flora chimes in, "You having a personal relationship might make it more difficult. Emotions are involved."

I wave a hand. "Normally, that doesn't apply to me. I

don't let my heart get tangled in operations. But I have to admit, this is different. It may be best if you two handle my mom."

The sound of music reaches my ears a block from my place, and I pull over and park.

I undo my seat belt and say, "I normally would call bullshit on my emotions being involved, but my mom being a protest leader has blunted my leadership skills. Without realizing it, I'm wondering what she's going to do next, or how she'll react."

I muse aloud, "I wonder what would my dad say about this weird situation if he were here?"

Vincent elbows me in the front seat. "You're too close. I could see it but didn't want to call you on it until now."

A headache throbs. Rubbing my temples, I say, "What do you guys suggest? Any ideas for how to approach this?"

Within minutes, we have a plan in place. We exit the car and close the doors quietly. I don't want to wake the neighbors, who are mostly retired folks who bought in the last few years, or alert the protesters that we're on our way.

Our waterfront town has attracted newcomers from big cities looking for the charms of small-town living. The trouble is, by hordes of them moving here, they're wrecking what they were seeking by increasing the popu-lation, building new homes, and remodeling, going up a floor for a better view. In the end, housing prices have skyrocketed, leaving locals scratching their heads about how to pay higher property taxes and wondering where their grown kids will find an affordable local place to buy or rent. It's a win for new folks, and a loss for long-timers.

I shrug off those thoughts as we move along the side-walk with stealth in the dark. We creep up on the crowd of about forty people gathered on my property. Three dome tents are pitched in the yard. Someone hung up a rope between two trees, and pants and shirts are hanging on it.

A bonfire blazes on the patio, of all places. My jaw drops. I just put in the paved area for holding four lawn chairs. I've got a fire pit farther from the house. Couldn't they have used that instead of burning logs on my new paid-for paved surface?

I grit my teeth and vow to set my mom straight when this is all over. I might even take her aside to talk some sense into her tonight. But I cock my head, doubting she'd listen. She never does.

Why do I continue to try to change her, when she is who she is? She's not going to become the mother I wanted, any more than I'll morph into the carefree daughter she yearned for. I thought we loved each other, despite our different views, but glancing around my prop-erty, I'm struck by how hopeless it is to try to shape her into someone different.

Vincent comes over to me and pats my shoulder. He whispers, "Remember, let us handle Daisy, and you'll check the house. If we need you, we'll let you know. Let's go."

I eye my back door, which is open a crack. I knew the

latch was loose, and my premises was vulnerable to intruders. I'd been meaning to replace it, but I was preoccupied with starting my own company and hiring my team. Finding my first client took all my time and focus.

I frown. There's no excuse for my not getting around to securing my house. I'm in the security business but ignored my own home's shortcomings. The word stupid comes to mind.

I step closer. The lights are on inside. In the kitchen, two people are making out and leaning against the counter. I shiver. The violation of strangers in my home crawls along my skin.

The reason I work so hard is because I am a nesting homebody, even though you wouldn't guess it by looking at me. I may look tough, but I want the comforts of home waiting for me after a long work day, or week, or month on the road.

My mouth hangs open when a guy in his early twenties jumps on my dining table. He stomps, keeping a beat only he hears. He must weigh two hundred pounds.

The table collapses, and he tumbles to the floor.

A minute later, he runs out of my house carrying pieces of the wood table I picked out at our local furniture store. He throws them into the roaring bonfire and grins. Thrusting his hands in the air, he dances around the fire.

My mother joins him, shaking her behind and hooting and hollering.

How heinous is her betrayal. How joyous she looks. She's laughing and smiling, all at my expense.

Her face is flushed. Her eyes are bright. She shimmies and shakes, stomping around the fire in a circle.

My stomach churns. She makes statements for peace but destroys my life. Doesn't she care about right and wrong? How could she harm her relative's property? What are these strangers thinking, coming here and breaking my things? Damn them all. We need to shut it down.

22

Before I go in my house I stop and observe my team in action. Flora and Vincent are going around telling people to vacate the premises. It helps that Vincent is built like a football linebacker, and Flora is fierce. From the look in her eyes, people know not to mess with her and her pointed fingernails.

The reggae music stops. Someone tosses a bucket of water on the fire. It sputters, and then roars back to life.

I nod. That's like my mother. She doesn't quit. She just keeps going, following her cause, no matter what. Fed by zeal and fueled by a fever to make things right. The problem is, we see different wrongs to correct from our vantage points.

The chasm is so wide, I realize now, as she waves her arms and protests to my staff, I don't know if we can close the gap. I shrug. Maybe I don't want to. Maybe it's time to let go of the longing I've lived with, wanting a loving, attentive mother. Leave the notion behind like baggage, dump it on the side of the road, and move on. I'll mull over what to do about her when the protest is over.

A man and a woman moan inside a tent. The tent fabric shudders, and ripples, and quivers. I roll my eyes. Great, just what I needed in my back yard.

As I turn to go into my violated house, they climax together. I'm tempted to cover my ears. I'm not a prude, but this is way over the top too much for my yard and my town.

This is my home, my safe place to retreat to when work gets tough. I've always felt secure here until now. Daisy brought these strangers along and violated my nest. If I were her, I'd conduct a ceremony later to clear the evil spirits by burning a stick of sage. But I'm too practical for that.

I leave Flora and Vincent to handle the group outside and turn to go into my home. I climb up the back steps. Someone used a crow bar to open the back door and splintered the wood on the door jam. I set my jaw and step into the kitchen.

The frig door is open. Cold air belches out. The appliance whines, as if this is too much of an affront.

A cupboard door is askew. It's been pulled off the hinge and dangles.

My hands fist.

Food remnants are strewn across the tile floor.

Someone stepped in smears of mustard and dollops of mayonnaise. I see shoe marks and skid marks, like someone slipped. Smashed slices of bread are scattered on surfaces. A can of tuna fish is open, with the lid up, but is otherwise untouched. A six-pack holder for beer lies on its side in the corner.

"Oh, my word," I say under my breath.

I will get revenge for this if it's the last thing I do. Moving on, I step into the living room. A woman in her mid-twenties is passed out on my red sofa, with a joint in her hands.

My hands clench. If she put burn marks in my upholstery, I'll hurt her until forever. I stride over and shake her by the shoulder. "Get out of here. Party's over."

She opens her eyes and squints at me. "Who are you? You can't tell me what to do. Daisy told us we could come here."

I swallow hard and force myself not to slap her across the face.

"Daisy is not in charge anymore. I am." I point to the front door. "Get out."

She stands and wipes a hand on her skin-tight jeans. Her boots cost a lot, I'd bet. Here she is, camping out at my place after breaking and entering, but it's not for lack of funds. She and my mother are cut from the same cloth.

I shake my head. They are takers, sponging off hard working people like me. With a reverse entitlement, they say, "I deserve your money because I'm better than you and making my voice heard, opposing your views. Give me a hand out. Lift me up. Give me your stuff. Open your home, whether you want to or not." How twisted is that?

I march to the front door and hold it open, gesturing for her to go. "I suggest you vacate the premises now. Or I'll conduct a citizen's arrest."

She snorts, and it's not a welcome sound. She says, "I'm staying here, no matter what. You can't tell me what to do. We're part of the free republic. We do what we want and go where we're called."

This is bullshit, but I clamp my mouth closed. No need to argue with someone who has a world view counter to mine so much there's no talking sense to them.

I pull a plastic zip tie from my pocket and dangle it in the air. "Your choice. I'll bag you and tag you. Or you can leave right now."

She grins and throws her head back, folding her arms. She has a triumphant glow about her, but I predict that is about to disappear in a quick minute.

In seconds, I'm at her side. I pull her wrists together in back and whip the zip tie around her wrists before she can react.

She shrieks and spits at me. "You have no right to do this."

I shove her to the door. "Oh, yes, I do. You're in my home, and that's breaking and entering. Let's go. You can join your friends."

I walk her down the front two steps and push her over to my team.

"Watch her, will you? I'll go back inside and check the rest of the rooms."

But as I turn to walk away, my mother marches over and grabs my hand, yanking hard. I pull out of her grasp and say, "Why are you wrecking my place? Don't you care?"

"You're my daughter. My friends and I should be able to camp here." She looks around and lowers her voice. "You're making me look bad in front of the others."

I stare at the woman who raised me with barely concealed resentment. "That's all you think about, isn't it? Since you came to town, you've been polishing your image. Trying to suck up to the leaders, so they consider you one of them."

She scuffs a shoe and studies the matted grass. Maybe she has a shard of sense and harbors a scintilla of shame for putting me in danger, wrecking my house and keeping my neighbors awake.

My heart is full of bitterness. I can't resist saying, "I was at that meeting, you know. At the protesters' planning meeting? I heard you give out my name and address and tell them when I worked. You put a target on my back. I'll never forgive you for that."

She pushes me on the chest and steps back. "And I'll never forgive you for ruining my life. I was happy with your father until you moved in with us." She stares at me and hisses, "He never told me about you until you arrived that day. Talk about a life-altering surprise on my birthday. And I can assure you, it wasn't a good one."

A wash of horror sweeps over me. The hairs on my arms stand on end. How could she be so cruel? I was just a kid. It wasn't my fault. But she's blaming me?

I clear my throat. This talk is toxic. I'll push away the hurt by taking a run and talking it over with a counsellor. "Your playtime with your group is over. It's ending now and not in five minutes. Because of what you've done, you're not welcome here. If this happens again, I'll call the police. You'll be removed from my property."

I turn to Vincent, who is standing by my side. "Zip tie her and the others. Send them packing."

He nods. "Got it, boss."

23

I cross my arms and frown. My mom and her friends are red in the face, standing in my yard, acting like they own the place. There must be fifteen or twenty of them.

Their hands are bound behind their backs. They struggle to free themselves, to no avail.

I go over to a couple snoring in a tent. "Pack it up. You're leaving right now."

Vincent joins me and claps his hands. "That's right. Your group is moving out. Let's go. Chop, chop."

They get up and gather their gear, grumbling the whole time.

"You can't do this," Daisy says, glaring at me. "I have a right to be here. You're my daughter. You don't treat loved ones like this."

I arch an eyebrow. Minutes ago, she accused me of ruining her marriage. No wonder I felt like an intruder in the house I grew up in. Now, to manipulate me and get her way and stay, she's acting like we come from a tight-knit family. I wish that was the truth.

The lack of love in my family made me turn to running to escape. I learned to hide my emotions, but I'm working on that. I want to rise to be a better person than where I came from.

With mixed emotions burbling away inside, I say, "Settle down, settle down."

I've got to get my mom and her pack of foolish hooligans gone. We need to be dealing with our client and not be side-tracked by my mother.

I'm about to send them in cuffs down the street to walk downtown, when the young woman who had slept on my red sofa speaks up.

She says, "How are we going to get these off our wrists?"

"My shoulders hurt," my mom says. "Cut these off, will you? Come on, Violet."

A twinge of guilt hits me before I brush it away. These people broke into my home not once, but twice. I'm not in the wrong. They are. Just because my mother is the leader of the pack doesn't make the situation any different than my team's usual approach to dealing with unlawful conduct.

I exchange a quick look with Flora and Vincent and say, "If you promise to leave peacefully and not come back, we'll cut the zip ties and let you go."

A moan goes up from the group.

I nod to Vincent, who says, "Or we can keep you here until the cops come to hail you off to jail."

Silence settles over my mom's followers.

Daisy steps forward. "Fine, cut these off, and we'll be on our way. But don't pretend you did us a favor. We have a right to occupy any premises we pick. Tomorrow, we will show you how wrong you were to tangle with us. We are strong. We are mighty."

No one repeats her mantra.

She turns to the others. "We are mighty. Isn't that right?"

"Yeah," a few say.

I give my mother a look that would scald a tomato. "You don't sound repentant or peaceful. Do you want to try that again? Are you going to leave here peacefully and not come back?"

She takes a long slow breath and glances at her followers. "Fine. Cut us free. You won't see us here again. You'll see our might downtown. We'll demonstrate and make news worldwide."

"That's right," the young man who broke my table says.

Ms. Red Sofa says, "We will prevail."

"Don't hurt everyday people with your cause," I say. "We're just like you, trying to pay the bills. Okay, guys, cut them free and let them go."

I slash the zip tie on the man who smashed my table and say, "You broke my table, and I'll have to replace it, thanks to you. You owe me a hundred bucks."

He laughs. "We're free agents. We don't carry cash. You're part of the system. I don't owe you anything."

A couple of curse words come to mind, but I don't reply. I press my lips together instead. No need to get into an argument now, not when they're supposed to be leaving. I want them out of my life and away from my house.

Vincent cuts my mom's hands free.

She rubs her wrists and turns to me. "You're in the wrong business. You should be working on our side and making the world a better place. Shame on you for being greedy and grabbing the money, instead of protecting the earth and workers who are being taken advantage of."

I shake my head slowly. "I guess we have different views, and this event has made it all clear we don't agree. My team and I aren't taking advantage of the workers. We are the workers. We're contributing to a cause to make it a better, safer world. What are you doing to really help others? It seems like you're doing this to enhance your own reputation and not for a greater mission to save the planet."

She spits on the ground. "What would you know about giving and helping? All I did was give, give, give when you lived with me. From day one, you took, took, took. And you didn't think about me or how it impacted me, did you?"

I sigh because she'll never understand. "I was a kid. I didn't ask to be left with you." I point down the street. "You and your group aren't welcome here. Get going."

Daisy's eyes narrow. "Then we'll see you tomorrow. You'd better get ready for the big jamboree. It's going to be a rocking time downtown."

I flinch. How large a scale of protest are they planning for tomorrow? Is our town prepared for what will take place? I worry that our meager police force is understaffed and out of practice for what's on the horizon.

Crossing my arms, I say, "Go on then. We'll handle whatever comes our way."

She turns to the hangers-on. "You heard my daughter. Let's go."

Ms Red Sofa says, "I'm tired. I want to sleep."

"It's only five blocks to downtown," my mom says.

As Daisy and her followers shuffle down the street, I marvel at how I've managed to not only defend my client's company but with civic pride, I'm acting like I'm defending the town. That's not my job, I remind myself. I need to stay in my silo.

Protect the client. Keep the team safe. That's my focus.

I'll deal with the mess in my house after this is all over.

My mom chants, "Stop polluting. Save the earth."

Her group marches away and repeats her words. "Stop polluting. Save the earth."

I turn to Vincent and Flora and wipe my brow. "Oh, man. That was crazy. I wonder what's in store for us tomorrow?"

24

Before we leave my house, I need someone to come over and stay for the rest of the night to secure the place, in case protesters return. Or my mom comes back. Or someone decides to take advantage of the broken back door.

I call my Uncle Fred to come over and watch the place. And then we set about cleaning the downstairs as best we can. Uncle Fred is an attorney, and he'll put the fear of God into anyone who tries to break in while I'm gone. He was my biggest supporter, along with his wife, Mary, when I was young. He always said if I needed him to call at any time of the day or night.

When I was ten, Daisy locked me out of the house for not loading and starting the dishwasher like she asked. I called my uncle and aunt, and they came to Olympia and took me out for ice cream until my dad picked me up.

Sadly, he brought me back to Daisy's wrath. She went on and on about how I didn't contribute to the household or do my chores after school.

My dad patted my knee as we drove to the house where I'd been dropped off like a package and dumped on the front step. He said, "Sorry about this, Vi, but we've all got to learn to adjust. We don't always get what we want."

I screwed up my face and wiped away tears as I stared out the window. He went by the marina and I gazed at a boat longingly. If only I could get on one of those and sail away and leave Daisy behind. But I wanted my dad with me.

Later, I recalled his words and wondered how he could be so wrong. He got what he wanted, by leaving Daisy and me for another woman. He dropped out of touch with me.

My mind snaps back to the present when Vincent says, "You write poetry?"

He holds up a few pages from those scattered across the living room floor.

I shrug. "Yeah, no big deal. We've all got to have a hobby, you know? When running doesn't take my mind off things enough, I turn to paper. It's not much."

My body is so beat with fatigue and my mind muddled from the confrontation with my mom that it takes a moment for me to realize where the poems came from.

My pulse picks up, and I race upstairs. My bedroom looks like a tornado hit it. Papers are strewn everywhere. Boxes have been pulled out of my closet. My private journal is open on the bedside table. My clothes are tossed on the bed.

I go closer and wrinkle my nose. A pair of red thong underwear is on my pillow. I grimace and almost gag. The word disgusting doesn't begin to describe what they did to my bedroom. I'm going to have to fumigate and renovate and wash it down with disinfectant.

Closing the door on the horrible spectacle, I clomp downstairs. Flora and Vincent are collapsed on the sofa with their eyes closed.

Vincent opens an eye. "What happened up there? Everything all right?"

I shake my head. "Nope. It's so bad, I don't want to talk about it."

"These people are pigs," he says, rubbing his eyes. "No boundaries. No respect for other people's things."

My uncle drives up. He steps out of his car carrying an overnight bag. His combover hair looks like a wind storm blew through it. I go out to greet him.

"Sorry I woke you," I say, guiding him into the house. "I really appreciate your doing this."

"No problem," he says.

When he steps into my place, his jaw drops. "What happened here?"

I glance at the yellow mustard smear on the wall. Written in red brown ketchup are the words, "You suck."

"My mom and some friends were here. They

destroyed the place. You're seeing it after we did a bit of cleaning. I'll have to re-paint the walls."

He nods. "I see. Daisy and her band did it. Your mother visits town and bring turmoil in her wake."

He wraps his arms around me and gives me a hug. "Honey, I'm sorry you're having to go through this. Daisy hasn't done you any favors, has she?"

I lean into his warmth. He's been more like the father I'd wished I'd had. For a moment, I'm a child again, but then I remember Vincent and Flora are watching us, so I step back and assume a leadership position.

"They broke down the back door, so the house isn't secure. I'm worried they might come back and camp out tonight, even though we sent them packing. The police weren't able to respond to my neighbor's call about the disturbance here.

Flora and Vincent stand and move to the front door.

Uncle Fred eyes the red couch. "Don't worry, I'll take care of it. I brought some reading to do while I wait, and I have a group of citizens ready to respond to a group text, if needed. We're like a neighborhood block watch, only different. Go back to the office, get some rest and be ready for tomorrow. We need someone to defend the town, because the police sure aren't doing it."

We raise our eyebrows and nod.

I say, "It's hardly fair to ask a police force this small to handle an event this big."

Uncle Fred says, "But they could have been better prepared."

"True." I turn to Vincent and Flora. "Shall we go?"

Vincent says, "We did the best we could cleaning up. I think you're going to have to call in professionals."

"I can handle it," I say.

A foul odor drifts past, and we look at each other.

I put my hands on my hips. "What is that smell?"

I march over to the hall closet and whip open the door.

Inside, a creature is curled up among the coats. It looks like they made a nest by pulling them off the wire hangers. I poke the being with my boot.

"Hey, are you alive?"

An arm rises. A groan follows. My favorite winter coat is pushed away.

"Get up," I say. "You're trespassing. Get the hell out of my house."

A teenage girl about the size of a waif yawns. "Where are the others? Who are you?"

"I'm the owner of this house. Daisy left. Get going, and don't come back. And you might want to take a shower in the near future."

She sniffs the air. "Yeah, I know. That's what my parents say. I'm going as long as I can just to bug them."

She stands and pulls down her black sweatshirt. "I've got to find the others. I want to join the anarchists on their next raid."

I look at the others. "Listen, kid, think about the consequences. If you do that, you'll be arrested and have a record."

She smiles, and her face looks angelic. But you never know from the way someone looks if they might be violent.

She opens her arms. "The anarchists have evaded arrest so far. They're making a point. People respect them. It takes a strong stance to get the public's attention."

She sounds like she's parroting lines she's been fed. "Listen, hon," I say, opening the front door. "Step back from the noise and pretend you're ten years older. Would you want an arrest on your record when you apply for jobs? Think about it. Don't follow the herd."

She says, "I'll get a job where that won't matter. I'll be a professional activist."

Pointing out the door, I say, "All right, then. We're all allowed our different views, as long as we don't harm each other in the process. There's the sidewalk. See you later."

She looks around. "I need to use the bathroom first."

"Nope, that option is closed. I've got hard and fast rules here. No strangers in the bathroom."

She wiggles her behind. "I really have to go."

I shove her out the door. "Bye, bye. See you later."

Her eyes flash, and she grabs her butt. "I think I just pooped my pants. I have this condition, you know."

I wave a hand in front of my nose. It certainly smells like she had an accident. I'm itching to kick her out because she broke into my place and leave her to find a port-a-potty downtown. I glance at Uncle Fred and gesture to the girl.

He says, "You've got things to do. Go on and get back to work. I'll let her use the bathroom while I'm here. It's what you would've wanted when you were her age."

I nod. He's right. The trouble is, I'm ticked off and want to take it out on someone. Daisy deserves the blame, and she's the one who should make restitution.

I say, "Just make sure she doesn't leave the bathroom in a mess like how her friends left it."

He turns to her. "Run in and take care of yourself. We'll have a talk afterwards."

I say, "Thanks, Uncle Fred."

"I'm always here for you, Violet," he says.

I give him a hug and lean into him, appreciating how he's here for me and making me feel safe.

As my team and I walk to my car to get back to business, I wipe a tear from my eye with the back of my hand. I'm lucky to be loved and cared for in the middle of this mess.

25

———

We head back to the office in my car. Commercial is blocked off by barricades, so I park in Old Town, and we walk the rest of the way. We glide along in silence, watching and assessing what's going on, looking for signs of unrest. We pass by Brinker's building. All is quiet. People are curled up in sleeping bags, snoring on the makeshift stage.

Closer to the office, a crowd of thirty or so gathers around a bonfire on Commercial. Two drummers thump on drums. A man leans against a wall in a vacant shop with broken windows. His mouth hangs open as he sleeps.

All is quiet, for now.

In the office, I take a quick shower and then crash on my cot in my office. I'm fully clothed and will jump up and take charge if the need calls.

"Night, guys," I say to Vincent and Flora, who elected

to stay over and sleep on cots in the bullpen instead of going home and returning a few hours later.

"Night," Vincent says.

"Night, night," Flora says in a soft voice.

"Get some shut eye," I call to the next room. "We'll be ready for whatever tomorrow brings."

I close my eyes and wonder if I'll be able to drift off with all that's going on in my mind. Daisy has made my life doubly difficult this week. The job is twice as tough with her fighting against me and riling people up. Recalling the sight of ketchup on my walls, I frown. Despite thoughts about my mother rankling me, sleep wraps a warm blanket over me, and I succumb.

IN THE MORNING, I grab a cup of coffee and eat a granola bar while I check the news at five a.m. I'm not going for a run, because I want to be on hand well before the protesters appear for their news conference at my client's office. I glance out an office window. A few people are up, but that's it.

Flora and Vincent are awake and dressed. They gulp down cups of coffee and check social media before we leave. We've worked together for long enough that we don't say a word. We just go about our business.

I wash out my cup and set it next to the sink to wash later. On my mug, given to me by Uncle Fred, it says,

"She's the best." I smile, fortified by his confidence in me, and hope all is well at my home.

At six a.m., I say, "Guys, let's gather for a quick word before we head out."

Flora clears her throat. "They're spreading word to meet at Bettermed's front entrance at seven a.m. today. Gather together to rock the world. Make a difference. That's what they're saying."

"They're expecting at least three television stations to show up," Vincent says. "And a reporter from the local paper and two papers in Seattle."

"Understood. And, remember, no engaging with the group. We'll let them be disappointed and drift away. The missing signs will come as a surprise to them, so we'll remain out of sight and blend into the background. We don't want to give the reporters something to write about by getting dragged into an argument outside the client's company."

Vincent grins. "Got it. Don't appear on the news. Stay behind the scenes."

I stretch my legs. I wish I could take a run now, but duty calls. The client matters most. I say, "Flora, how do the feeds from the surveillance cameras look?"

"Relatively quiet. A few people are on benches outside the post office. It's a ghost town at the client's building. No action yet."

Mimi comes in and hangs up her coat.

"Good to see you," I say. "How's it looking out there?"

She shrugs. "Everyone is sleeping or just waking up. The streets are a mess. Trash everywhere."

"So much for tending to Mother Earth, I guess." I shrug on my jacket. "We're taking off, and I'm not sure when we'll be back. Might be ten or eleven or more like noon."

"Go get 'em," she says. "I'll let you know if the mayor's staff or police reach out."

I zip up my coat and pull on a knit cap. "I thought about texting them this morning with an update, but I decided not to. It's a wasted effort. I warned them ahead of time, and they didn't listen. Surely, they must have their own ears to the ground by now."

I put a hand on the door and turn back to her. "On second thought, why don't you call our contacts at the police and fire departments and city hall? Tell them we've heard it's going to be gnarly today. They need to anticipate a riot."

Mimi grins. "Gnarly? You want me to say that?"

I chuckle. "You can skip that part and tell them we've heard the protesters say today will be a raging storm like the town has never seen before. Buckle down and brace yourselves. It's going to get wild."

26

Vincent, Flora, and I leave the office and hustle down the stairs. I want to move my legs and get the circulation going to clear my mind. Outside, people climb out of dome tents. Purple tents, green tents, and yellow ones sit on the sidewalk like mushroom caps. A man with stringy hair yawns with his arms raised. When I see his hairy belly and a navel piercing, I look away. A middle-aged woman in pajamas stumbles out of a tent and brushes her teeth on the street. Downtown has turned into one big bedroom this morning.

We turn the corner and stride down Commercial, heading for the client's building.

As we move ahead, I'm relaxed. I did my best to prepare for the protesters' press conference. Now, we'll watch and see how it plays out.

I say to Vincent and Flora, "So far, we've been lucky. The client's offices haven't been vandalized. No windows have been broken, and, fortunately, no employees roughed up. But if things go upside down in the next few hours, and they try to destroy the building or break inside, we'll have to intervene."

Flora's jaw tenses. She says, "I'm ready."

I scan the streets. "I don't see a police presence yet."

Vincent says, "It's a bit early. They might still be at the Donut House."

I chuckle and say, "We've got to stop ribbing them. They're doing their best. It's not the officers' fault they didn't have enough manpower yesterday. I'd say that responsibility and blame rests on the chief of police's shoulders. It'll be interesting to see how people in town feel about the police chief and city hall after the protesters leave and this is over."

Vincent says, "I have a feeling they're not going to be happy about how this was handled."

"I agree," Flora says.

We stop at the back entrance to the Bettermed building, and a guard buzzes us in. With the trade meetings in mind and the threat Brinker received, I called in security guards to provide extra coverage and watchful eyes.

Brinker is pacing the lobby when we walk in. His face is pale, and he has dark smudges under his eyes. I get the feeling none of us have slept well for the last few days.

He wrings his hands and says to me, "I'm nervous

about this. Are you sure a strategy of do not engage is the best approach?"

I nod. "Definitely. We've had close contact with this group, including a confrontation last night. There's no win in it if you argue with them in public. They don't want to change their opinions, just like we don't. They want to make a splash and attract media attention and grow their followers."

He scratches his stubbled chin, where silver and gray and black whiskers show.

I say, "They'll come here, find the signs gone, and fade away. Nothing to see, no news here, move on." Out of the corner of my eye, I see a news truck pull up and park outside. "Mr. Brinker, I suggest you go into your office and don't appear visible in the lobby or at a window. I don't want an image of you shown on television that makes you look like you're cowering inside your building. Go, and we'll take care of it."

He blows out a breath and nods. "Point taken. I'll go to my office and see if I can get anything done. Keep me updated."

"We will." As he walks away, I say to the security guard, "Are the doors locked?"

He stands from his seat behind the front counter. "Yes."

"If calls come in to the main line, do not respond to questions. Tell them you'll take a message."

"Understood." He scratches his arm and glances out

the front door. With large rectangular glass panes, we have a clear view outside. "Do you think the crowd is going to break in? I'm not prepared for that."

Vincent says, "We don't expect that'll happen. We've taken measures to de-escalate the situation. We expect the group will disperse."

The guard presses his lips together. "But if they don't, what will we do? Call the police? I heard they weren't responding to calls yesterday. They were too busy. I have a family to consider. I can't get hurt."

I say, "If that happens and rioters manage to run inside, you have my permission to duck under the desk, if you need to, for your own safety."

"Oh, good," he says, studying the floor. Looking up at me, he says, "I just took the job so I could study for college classes while on the job and get paid for it. I didn't expect unrest, just a quiet, boring guard job."

"Believe me, we didn't either. The town has been turned upside down by protesters."

Another TV truck parks across the street.

"This would be a good time for a bio break," I say, "if anyone needs one. It might be a while until the next opportunity."

My hands are clammy. I count my steps as I move down the hall to the restroom to keep my mind busy. Stay calm, I tell myself.

I leave the bathroom without checking the mirror. No need to see how haggard I look after so little sleep and so much stress. If only my mother hadn't come to town. It would've been easier if my relative wasn't on the other side of the issue.

By the time I get back to the lobby, about fifteen people are gathered outside at the front entrance. My eye catches on a woman wearing an orange caftan, and I wince. My mother is out there, intent on raising hell.

I go over to Vincent and say, "I hope the changes we made last night will thwart their plans this morning. They've built this up as a major event. It would be great if the news crews drifted away, and they didn't get much media coverage."

More protesters gather outside the Bettermed building. News crews set up. People with cameras on their shoulders march around out front.

I say to Vincent and Flora, "One of us should be out there and listen to what they're saying. It might as well be me."

Vincent's eyes grow wide. "Isn't that a risk? She knows you. Your being there might aggravate the situation."

I cross my arms. "I've never shied away from conflict, so I'm not going to stay in here and hide just because my mom is in charge. I want to hear it first-hand, but I'll stand back aways."

He cocks his head. "Okay, but it might not be the best idea. We'll stay inside and monitor the video feed. Text me if things are about to explode, and we'll barricade Mr. Brinker in his office."

It might not be the wisest decision I've ever made, but I can't resist being on the scene in person and watching my mom in action. I slip out the back door and saunter around to the front, doing my best to blend in. I'm just a nobody, checking out the scene. No need to notice me or point me out as a potential threat.

I lean against the wall. With my boots and jeans and oversized denim jacket, I could be anyone from the other side. I whip out a baseball cap, slap it over my head, and study the sidewalk.

A breeze brushes past my cheek. I shove my hands in my pockets and pull out my phone to be ready to text my team.

I glance at the stage. It's empty. All the energy is focused on the front entrance of my client's building.

A reporter in a TV station blue rain jacket and long brown hair walks from a news truck. She has a microphone in her hand. A camera man follows her. She glances at the front entrance of the building.

With a shrug, she says to the camera man, "No news if we don't have a visual image for viewers to focus on. That wall is bare. It looks like any other wall in the area."

I bite the inside of my check and suppress a smile.

The reporter and camera man turn and walk away.

My mom calls out, "Wait, don't go. We're about to make an announcement."

The news crew stores their gear in the truck and drives off.

Holding a megaphone to her mouth, my mom says, "We're here today to protest the questionable practices of technology companies like this one. Bettermed is among the worst offenders in ignoring what's best for individuals. Their exorbitant prices end up hurting people who pay the bills as patients in hospitals and long-term care facilities."

Folks in the crowd nod. A few people yawn. A man sips from a coffee thermos mug. A woman in her forties with red hair holds up a phone and records the event.

I shift my weight to the other foot. I'm looking casual, like someone listening on the side lines.

The group has grown to twenty-five or thirty people.

"This company here," my mom says, pointing to the front door, "is hosting the trade association talks. They need to shut down the discussions. Let's put an end to people in power making decisions for us. Let's stop the meetings!"

"Stop the meetings," people say in monotone voices.

Daisy shouts, "We're in charge. We're taking back our power."

Onlookers repeat her words in faint voices. A grizzled older man sways from side to side. People walk away. Perhaps the time of day is too early for enthusiasm.

The waif-like teenage girl from my front hall closet is standing in back. She looks at me and glances away, fixating on what my mother is saying. Her face is clean, and she looks like she managed to get cleaned up at my place while Uncle Fred protected the premises. Uncle Fred is the best.

Daisy motions with her hand. "Come on, let's give it up for truth and justice. Let me hear you roar. Stop the meetings."

Twenty weak voices say, "Stop the meetings."

Stragglers drift away. Fifteen people remain.

A lone anchorwoman from Channel 5 steps up to my mom. "Which company is this? I don't see a sign."

Daisy points at the front door. "This is Bettermed's headquarters."

The reporter cocks her head. "Where's the sign? We need to show that in our footage."

Daisy shrugs. "I guess they took it down last night." She says to the reporter, "Aren't you going to ask me questions and interview me?"

The reporter shakes her head. "There's no news here. And are you aware the trade talks ended early? The delegates left town yesterday afternoon."

The camera man isn't holding up the camera or recording the conversation.

My mom looks over a dwindling group of ten or so people. "We're still going to protest and make a scene in town today. We'll show the world that the environment matters. Corporations shouldn't make decisions that hurt regular folks without our having a say."

The reporter eyes my mom, as if she's deciding whether to get a sound bite from her. "What is your occupation and your interest in this?"

My mom's chest swells up, and she stands taller. "I'm an organic farmer."

"You don't represent an official group?"

Daisy shrugs. "No, I don't. I'm just here volunteering my time for a good cause."

The reporter nods and says to the camera man, "This was a bust. Let's go back to the station."

As they get in a news van, my friend Ned comes over and talks to Daisy while taking notes. She's busy with her interview, so I slip away and head to the back entrance.

I'll talk to Ned later. I can't be the voice for Brinker and his company. That wouldn't be appropriate. I also don't want to confront my mother in front of a member of the media and have our personal crap pasted all over news outlets. That would be mortifying, if that happened.

Inside, I brief Brinker on what happened out front.

"The group wasn't huge, and it's dispersing. The only reporter who was interested in the story is from Seattle. But I doubt she'll cover the press conference. There isn't much to write about."

He shakes my hand and smiles. "Violet, I can't thank you enough. I really appreciate how you handled this."

I shrug, like it's no big deal, even though it's stressed me and my team out. "Glad to help your company."

He nods. "Thank you. I'll speak to others I know in the

Chamber of Commerce when this mess ends. I'm sure you'll get new clients out of this."

A flutter of joy tickles my belly. This could be the making of my company. After this, we'll be set for clients, and I won't have to go network at the Chamber of Commerce to drum up business.

"Thank you, sir. I appreciate that."

He says, "You really should join the Chamber of Commerce, you know. Meet other like-minded business owners. I think you'd enjoy getting to know them. I'm in it, and I'll introduce you."

I resist the urge to roll my eyes. The last thing I want to do is sit in a stuffy meeting room with straight-laced squares, hearing boring presentations and eating rubber chicken for lunch. But something about his suggestion tugs at me.

He may be right. It could be a good idea. I could use the support. Maybe the other business owners in Millersville aren't as different from me as I suspect.

"Thanks, I think about it."

28

I walk out of Brinker's building and take a moment to pause and breathe the sea air coming off Cedar Channel. The air is still. You'd never know a protest storm is building. From what my mother said last night and implied this morning, there will be trouble in town today.

Although we take pride in our clean town, trash is strewn around. Women and men of all ages stumble out of dome tents. Their clothes are rumpled, but the line at the coffee shop is out the door and around the corner.

I walk past a line of porta potties and wrinkle my nose. At least the mayor got that right. People need a place to do their business. We don't want bare butts hanging out over the curb, dropping brown gold, as a plumber told me, on the street like I saw in Seattle one time.

A woman with round cheeks and brown curly hair

comes out of a porta potty. The door slams shut. "No toilet paper," she says. "It's disgusting in there. What a mess. You're next?"

I raise my eyebrows. "Nope, just passing by. Have a good day."

I'm a few feet past her when she says, "Say, aren't you Daisy's daughter? The one she talks about?"

My shoulders slump, and I turn around. I might as well acknowledge the family tie. No need to be rude to a stranger who means well.

"Yeah, she's my mom."

The woman chuckles. "It's weird you're working against each other on opposite sides. She talks about you a lot, and it sounds like she loves you. I don't know if you knew that."

I sigh and scuff my boot on the pavement. It rained last night, and the street glistens with moisture. A puddle is right by my foot, and I tap the sole of my boot on the surface of the water while I think. How could someone thwart me, and threaten me, and yet love me?

"I hadn't realized that," I say.

"Sounds like she may have some regrets about the way she raised you," the stranger says. "No one is perfect."

I let out a sigh. "No, we're not. Thanks for telling me. See you around."

As I turn to go, she says, "Just an inside tip, it might be best if you stayed away from town today at noon. Things are going to ramp up and get violent. But don't tell anyone

I said that. I'm just passing it along because you seem nice, and Daisy cares about your safety. She told me to pass it on if I ran into you."

Striding down a side street to the office, I ponder the mystery of how my mom could care about me and yet trash my home. Is it possible in any version of reality for her to love me and be cruel to me? For her to want to protect me and keep me safe while wreaking havoc and bringing trouble to town?

I'm not sure, but the idea intrigues me. Duality lies deep within each of us. The good and the bad. The loving and the angry. Somehow though, I hadn't expected that of the woman who raised me.

My phone dings with a text. My friend Ned wants to interview me for an article she's working on about the protests.

I shake my head and continue to the office. No way I'll agree to that. My job calls for me to stay under the radar. I'm not a feature for folks to fixate on. I'm the one in the background, guaranteeing my client's safety and security.

I text back. "I can't. You'll have to find someone else."

My phone rings, and I duck into an alley and lean against a brick wall. Three people are huddled together and talking a way down, gesturing with waving arms. They look like they're planning something.

Ned is calling, and because we're friends, I don't let it go to voice mail. I answer my phone in a muffled voice. "I'll call you back in a few minutes."

A big man with wild eyes and uncombed long brown hair says, "A big explosion is what we need. We need to blow up the refinery to make a statement."

A middle-aged woman with a pony tail shakes her head. "Security is tight there. I doubt we could get close enough. Besides, we might get burned in the fire."

"Good point," says a gray-haired man with a pointed chin. He pushes his wire-rimmed glasses farther up on his nose. "We need a target closer to town anyways. The protests are here. It makes more sense if we hit a building in Millersville."

The trio quiets for a moment.

I swallow hard and scroll on my phone, pretending not to listen. I pull on my ball cap visor to better cover my face. When they start talking, I glance over out of the corner of my eyes.

"Of course, the police would expect us to hit the building where the trade meetings were held," the woman says. "We need to pick somewhere else and surprise them. I want to leave my mark on this event. The protest of the decade."

Mr. Glasses says, "How about one of those ships by the docks? I've heard trucks fill them up with refinery by-products. We'd show them and make a statement about dependence on oil, right near ground zero at the protests."

The woman touches his elbow. "Jack, that won't work. It'd blast toxic sulfur all over the protesters. There's got to be a better way."

The big guy taps a finger to his lips. "How about we hit the Port shed? We could start a fire there and attract attention. It's old and made of wood. I bet it'd burn in a minute. Wouldn't that be a sight? Like Fourth of July fireworks only better."

"Yeah," say the other two.

Mr. Glasses says, "We've got it."

The woman says, "Let's not tell Daisy or Ralph. They might squash the idea."

The big guy says, "It's our secret."

I scuttle away and speed dial the police chief. His assistant puts me on hold. Grating canned music plays. I grit my teeth and hustle up the stairs to the Outrigger offices, puffing hard with each step.

My whole body is on alert because of what I learned in the alley. My fingers tingle as I grip the phone. My nose flares. As I barge into the office, the chief of police comes on the line.

Mimi looks up at me.

I hold up an index finger and head to my office.

"Violet," the chief says. "What've you got for me? My assistant said it was important."

I pace the room. "Sir, I just learned some protesters are planning to set fire to the Port shed at noon today. I thought you'd like to know. Perhaps you can stop it from happening."

He says in a drawn-out voice, "Now where did you hear that? No one else has mentioned it." He chuckles. "I bet it's just idle chatter. You're getting too worked up about the protests. Apart from an isolated incident with a few anarchists breaking windows, they seem to be a peaceful group."

"Sir, I beg to differ. How do you think the business owners feel about their windows getting broken and stores ransacked? I don't think they feel the same way you do, having to guard their stores all night."

"I wouldn't be so concerned. But thanks for letting me know."

He hangs up, and I set the phone down on the desk. I'm tempted to throw it against the wall, but that would only hurt me and wouldn't help the situation. The man is a total idiot.

I glance out the window. More people are gathering on the street. The crowd has grown since yesterday.

My heart thumps. It's going to be a blow out, and I need to alert my team.

29

I stand before my team in the office and say, "We thought we had events nailed. But I just learned there's a plan to light the Port shed on fire at noon today. That's near Bettermed, so we've got to take preventive measures to protect his property."

Mimi's mouth drops open. "Did you tell the police chief about that? What did he say?"

I sigh. "He blew it off and said it was just idle chatter. He didn't see it as a threat."

"Oh, man," Mimi says, running a hand through her hair. "Any way we can track the people who are planning this and stop them?"

I give my crew a description of the three individuals in the alley and tell them what I heard. "Let's be on the lookout for these people and keep our eyes open. Mimi, will you alert the fire department, in case this turns out to be real? I'll let Brinker know."

A chill runs up my spine. Just when I thought we were approaching the finish line, it moved farther away. Will the week ever be over?

I look my staff in the eyes and say, "It's going to be a tough day, but we can do this. Cover your assignments and plan to meet at the Brown later today. We'll hoist a beer and toast to our success."

Mimi folds her arms. "We'll see you there."

I call Brinker, and we talk about what I heard. He says he'll vacate the building and leave the security guards in charge.

When I hang up from talking with him, my phone rings. It's Ned.

I answer, and she says, "I thought you were going to call me back?"

I swallow hard. I don't have time to chat, not now, with the whole town about to burn down. "Something came up. Sorry about that."

She says, "We need to meet. I want to hear your side of the story. So far, I've only spoken with your mother and gotten her comments on record. She said some juicy sound bites about your relationship."

My eyes pop open, and I say in a loud voice, "What?"

I glance at the bullpen. Vincent is looking at me.

I wave off his concern and say to Ned, "I don't have time to talk, and I told you I didn't want Daisy's and my relationship to be the focus of an article about events in town."

"My editor is keen on including you in the story. It's about the protests but with a human-interest angle. It'll be focused on family, with quotes from you and Daisy. She told me all about when you were growing up in much more detail than you've told me, by the way. It makes for riveting reading."

I groan and lean my forehead against the cool window glass. How on any planet can this be happening? How did my mother manage to make herself a leader of the protests and be featured in a story that will expose my personal life? The situation is surreal.

My temples throb. I've gone to great lengths to shove my personal life and my childhood out of the spotlight. Until this week, I haven't spoken to my staff about my family. Now the story is about to be busted open and shown to gawkers and lookie-loos reading the news.

I roll my eyes. Great, let's expose Violet's secret past and toss out salacious morsels for strangers to mull over and discuss. I gulp. This is not what my new business needs.

Ned says, "I want you to tell your side of the story, so it's not just about her. How do you feel about your mom being on the opposite sides of the issue? It'll made a great basis for a story."

My face heats. My fingers drum on the windowsill. Ned is setting me up for public embarrassment. My reputation as an expert in providing security services for clients will crash. I'll be exposed in the press and hounded by more reporters. I'm an introvert who is driven to deliver results, and my strange family life being flashed across the news is the last thing I want. Who would sign on with someone whose own mother was visibly working against her?

Ned says, "If I have to, I'll go to press without presenting your side of the story. We're publishing it online in an hour. If you want to add your comments and voice your views, we have to meet right away."

My heart hammers, telling me to run and hide. But I can't. I don't want to talk to Ned, but I must. I need to control the narrative. Daisy opened the chasm I'm about to fall into, and I must set the record straight on my behalf.

"Fine," I say. My hands sweat as I grip the phone. Without considering the consequences, I say, "Let's meet at Gigi's Café. They have the best scones. I'll see you there in ten minutes."

30

Gigi's Café is located in an old two-story house a few blocks from downtown. I head over there, walking at a fast clip, and go past a tall maple tree, and up a ramp. Stepping inside, I inhale the powerful, welcome smell of fresh ground coffee and baked scones. Digging into a warm buttery scone is what I need to take the edge off a hectic week.

A crush of people are seeking a morning fix of carbohydrates and caffeine, and every table is taken. Two middle-aged women get up from their seats as I look around the café. I break out in a smile and wave to them. Shawna has a ready smile and curly brown hair. Ms. Pink is in her usual workout outfit of a pink sweatshirt and matching sweat pants. I met them when their book group was trapped in a barn by my previous employer.

They wave back and come over to me.

"Violet," Shawna says, wrapping her arms around me and giving me a hug.

I pat her on the back. "Did you recover from your ordeal yet?"

Her face flushes. "Yes, and I never want to do that again."

I turn to her friend. "Ms. Pink, what's up? Anything exciting happening lately?"

Ms. Pink grins. "Not since we last saw you."

Shawna says, "We've got to run. We're going on a guided bird walk." She smiles. "But if you ever need a part-time crew, think of us. We can handle anything after what we went through."

I nod. "You were tough. I'll keep it in mind. See you later."

I glide over to the table and grab the two-top before anyone else comes in. The town is hopping, and I'm lucky to get a seat at one of our busiest spots. Karina, the new owner, is a young woman in her mid-twenties. She moved home from Seattle when her grandmother's health was failing, and Karina took over running the cafe.

I nod to Karina, who is wiping a forearm across her brow.

She comes over to my table and says, "Violet, isn't it? I'm Karina. My grandmother told me you've become a regular customer since you were hired by that biotech company on the outskirts of town. But I guess they went belly up? I read about it in the paper."

I give her a long look, studying her face. The fact that Karina happens to be my secret half-sister makes me curious about her. Are we alike because we share the same father? Do we have the same tastes in clothes and food preferences? Someday I'll gather the courage to talk with Karina about our being related, but I'm not ready to yet.

I take in her pink hair, black leather pants, and pierced nose. She seems like a solid person, and someone I wouldn't mind being associated with. Besides, her scones are the best around and as good as her grandmother's.

I shake her hand and appreciate her firm grip.

I say, "That's right. Nice to meet you. I opened my own firm recently and hired my old team. We'll be spending a lot of time here, I bet. By the way, I'm sorry to hear about Gigi's passing."

Her eyes glisten with tears, and she looks down. "I never expected it. Her death came as such a surprise to me and my aunt. We thought she'd live forever. She was such a strong woman. Nothing stopped her."

She wipes her eyes and sniffs.

I have a lot I could say on that topic, but I hold off. She doesn't need to hear me opine on how death is like a boat taking us down a river, and we have no control. Who knows when the end will come for any of us? It could be in a minute, or tomorrow, or next year, or decades from now. I try to keep that in mind and appreciate each moment I'm alive, while I keep an eye out for the grim reaper to fend it off. Danger lurks in unexpected places, like on Millersville's streets, and in my house, and on my land amid the protests. If I can avoid it, I will.

Karina says, "What'll you have?"

"A black coffee for me, two scones with butter and jam, and a soy milk latte for my friend, Ned, who is on her way."

Her eyes light up. "Ned's coming? Great." A flicker of concern crosses her face. "We're fresh out of soy milk, and we don't serve lattes or cappuccinos. Just straight, black coffee with creamer on the side, if you must."

I lift my eyebrows. "Talk about bucking trends and keeping it old-fashioned."

She nods. "It's what Gigi wanted, but who knows, someday I might get with the times. It would make a lot of noise in here though, don't you think? And make conversation difficult?"

I glance around. "You're right. It's loud in here with people talking, and the sound bounces off hard surfaces, like the wood floors and walls. What does Ned usually order when she comes in?"

Karina says, "She asks for a black coffee with two sugars. I'll get right on it." She slips behind the counter to prepare our order.

Ned slides into the seat across from me and sets her phone on the table. Her pink phone cover sparkles. "Glad you snagged a table. Seems like everyone is in town right now and at the best spot for scones."

"Good to see you," I say, "although I wish it was under different circumstances. Let's get started, so I can get this over with."

Ned looks over at Karina and back at me. "Has anyone ever told you that you and Karina look a lot alike? It's amazing. You have the same nose, the same high hairline, the same defined cheekbones."

My throat closes tight. I don't want Ned or anyone to find out my secret, not before I have a chance to speak with Karina alone about what I learned long ago in a hidden letter in the attic. I'd recognize my dad's handwriting anywhere. It was a rainy day, and my mom was at a rally, protesting property tax increases at the state capitol for the day.

I crept up the fold-down attic steps and tugged on the metal pull cord to turn the bare light bulb on. And then I spied the dusty trunk. Opening it, I found some documents and among them, a letter from my dad to a woman in Millersville acknowledging he had another daughter named Karina Walker. Apparently she'd sent it back, because she'd written on the back of his letter and underlined the words, "I don't want money. I just thought you should know. Please don't contact me again."

My hands trembled, and the letter floated out of my hands onto the floor. I let out a low whistle, shoved the paper in the trunk, and slammed the lid, locking away the news. But it clung to me like the cloying smell of cooking oil.

I'd thought I was special. But the letter burst my bubble. I wasn't his only Daddy's girl, his special flower. As I climbed down the steps to the main floor, a thought occurred to me. Now I knew there were two of us. But were there others? And if so, how many daughters and sons did my father have?

That was the day I started jogging, when I was fourteen years old. I wanted to run away from the news I'd never wanted to know. I glance at Karina.

My dad's other daughter is in the same room with me, but I doubt she knows about our bond. I've developed a habit of coming to Gigi's, and I'm addicted to her scones. Although I'm afraid to face a family secret and broach the topic with Karina, I won't avoid her café.

Ned waves a hand in front of me. "Hello? Anybody home? Looks like I lost you there for a minute."

I take a deep breath. "Yeah, I got sidetracked, but I'm with you now. What questions do you want to ask?"

Ned pulls her blond hair back in a ponytail and rolls up her sleeves. She sets her phone to record, and we begin.

31

———————

Karina brings over two cups of coffee and sets down two scones. I'm glad for the interruption, because it gives me a reprieve from beginning the interview with Ned. My stomach knots. The baked goods smell appealing, but I've lost my appetite.

I take a sip of hot coffee and lean forward, my elbows on the table. I'd rather be anywhere else, but this is the right course of action. I'll say a few words and head back to the team to prepare for the possible fire and whatever else the protesters have planned. I raise an eyebrow, realizing Ned may have information about my mother's plans that will help me thwart whatever she and the others concocted.

I hold up an index finger. "Before we start, what did Daisy tell you? I'd like to know, so I can respond."

Ned checks her notes. "She said it was difficult to love someone and yet oppose them on issues. That you were a leader from the time you arrived at her house."

I rub my forehead. This is getting too personal to splatter across the page of a newspaper. I set down the coffee cup and push it away. "She mentioned that? I don't want that in the article."

Ned tilts her head. "It's her statement, so it's not up to you. But you can counter it if you like."

I swallow hard. "What did she say about why she's in town? And what are they going to do today? Did she mention that?"

Ned pats the table. "I can't divulge that. Let's get back to you. When did you realize your mother was one of the ones in charge of the protest?"

I squirm in the hard, unforgiving chair. When I've been in the café before, the seats didn't feel so uncomfortable. Putting off answering, I pick at my chapped lips. I'm more of a doer than a divulger, so this is difficult. I decide not to tell Ned I attended the protester planning meeting, because that would be giving away a trade secret about infiltrating and intelligence gathering.

I let out a slow breath and say, "I guess when I saw her on a bench in front of the post office, speaking into a megaphone."

"And how has this affected you and your work?"

"I don't think it has, really. I'm doing the same job of

protecting a client that I've always done." Realizing this is an opportunity to make a plug for my company, I add, "My company, Outrigger Services, is the best in the business of providing security services. Each team member is skilled in intelligence gathering and providing the full array of protective services. We've worked together for a long time."

Ned says, "And where was that?"

I give her a smile, because she knows the answer to that. She's just asking to put it on the record for the article. "Chaos Corporation, a biotechnology company that was located in the area."

She glances at her notepad. "I'd like to know a bit more about how you came to be in this business. Did you follow in your father's footsteps and join the military? Your mother mentioned that."

I sigh, wondering what else Daisy has said that will appear in print.

Karina comes by just then and refills our coffee. She has an easy manner, and I feel she is a kindred spirit. Maybe when I speak with her, it won't be as awkward as I imagined. But that won't be for a long time. I'm putting work first, and my new company calls for all my attention these days.

Karina pauses, coffee pot in hand. "You were in the military? Thank you for your service."

I nod. "I joined the Army right out of high school."

Karina leaves, and Ned says, "And you grew up where?"

"Near Olympia." I think back to the one-story two-bedroom house on an arterial and how my dad kept the temperature low to save on heating bills. I was always cold, despite wearing heavy sweaters bought from Goodwill or sitting under a blanket.

A shiver runs through me, and I stand. "I'm sorry, but I've got to go back to the office. It's a busy time for us."

Ned looks surprised. She tucks her notepad in her bag and puts away her phone, which has been recording the conversation. "Thanks for making time to meet with me."

We pay at the counter and split the bill.

Karina says, "Is Daisy, one of the protest leaders, your mother?"

"That's right," I say, figuring I might as well be open about it. Soon, it'll be splashed all over the news. "She's always rallied for causes and likes to stir people up. But I think this is the first time she's been one of the ones in charge."

Karina drums her fingers on the counter. She has short nails, and I've heard she's a potter and a painter. I don't know how she finds time for that and to handle the shop.

She says, "Did she have to pick a protest right here where you live? Talk about putting it in your face. It must be difficult for you."

I squinch up my face and nod.

Karina says, "I heard you're providing security services for Mr. Brinker's company. I know his daughter, Boots. She admires you and says you're tough and decisive."

Ned scribbles down notes.

"Thanks, but anyone in my position would be like that." With a shrug, I decide to answer Karina honestly. Nothing can hurt me now. My mom is open about me being her daughter. I might as well own it and engage in conflict. Don't shy away. Move to the threat and disarm.

I say, "It's been a tough the last few days, but we're almost at the end of the protests. Hopefully by the end of today, it'll be over, and we can tell stories about it over coffee."

Karina hands me back my credit card. "I heard the protesters who were hauled away on buses and jailed are out on bail. A guy in here earlier said they're expected back in town any minute."

I stuff the credit card in my wallet. "Thanks for the info. I've got to get going."

She glances at our table. "Do you want me to wrap up your scone to take with you?"

"I'll tuck it in a napkin, thanks," I say. "Good to see you. Maybe we can get together some time."

Karina smiles. "I'd like that. I don't have many friends here. Everyone left after high school, but I came back."

Ned points at the two of us. "You're both small business owners. And you have the same nose. You have a lot in common."

Karina gives me a close look and touches her nose. "You've got the same bump, in the same place."

My pulse quickens. "Weird, huh? Well, got to go. See you later."

Marching outside, my armpits prickle with sweat. I'm not ready to confront Karina or talk about who our father was. Besides, I could be wrong, and maybe the letter was about someone else. Did I misunderstand it? No, I read it several times that day to be sure of what it said.

Ned says, "Where are you off to in such a hurry?"

I pause on the sidewalk. I won't tell her about the possible fire at the Port shed. The trio might have been tossing out ideas with no intention of following through. Besides, if it happens, she'll hear about it.

"We have a staff meeting at the office. Got to head back."

"See you later."

As she walks in the other direction, toward her motel across from the dog park, I consider how our lines of work are similar but different. We're both in the business of chasing fires. While she reports on them, I do my best to prevent violence and smother flames of unrest.

I shove the heavy scone in my pocket and frown, reminded of my mother. If only Daisy wasn't stirring up trouble and talking to reporters. She didn't have to mention my childhood to Ned. I don't know if I can ever forgive Daisy for demolishing the wall I built around my private life, leaving me exposed and vulnerable.

The sound of drumming vibrates through the air as I stride to the office. It's louder than yesterday. The beats are insistent, as if the drummers are angry and issuing a warning.

I shiver and hurry ahead.

32

—————

Mimi and Flora and I stand in the bullpen briefing each other. Vincent is monitoring activities at Bettermed. Shouts outside make us rush to the windows. We're curious, and we want to see the spectacle first-hand, not from a camera feed on a computer monitor.

Women and men of all ages are marching side by side in an endless procession. They're carrying signs and banners. Drums hammer out a beat.

Goosebumps prick my flesh.

"Awe inspiring, isn't it?" I say to Mimi.

She blows out a breath. "It's quite the turnout."

Flora says, "They did a good job getting the word out about this event."

Mimi scratches her chin. "That's the beauty of social

media. Put it out there, ask people to share it, and watch it spread like wild fire."

"I heard someone on the street say," Flora adds, "they were from New York City. Another was from Buenos Aires."

I say, "They all came to prove a point. You have to hand it to them. They know what they're doing and how to gather support."

"I agree," Mimi says. "Our opposition has a well-planned playbook. My concern is for it not to turn dangerous today."

Flora nods. "With so many people squeezed in together, violence is likely to break out."

I recall how I promised the woman with the shoe store on Commercial that we'd shop there. "I told a shop owner we'd come by and buy pairs of her high-end running shoes. She was super upset when the anarchists busted her window last night."

Flora purses her lips. "Poor woman. Sure, I'll shop there."

Mimi says, "Is that the one across from the post office?"

"Yep."

"Count me in," she says.

Down on the street, two men in their twenties run over to a porta potty and push it over. They throw their fists in the air and scream. Enthusiasm, energy, and violence, along with a zealot's passion, are present, mixing in a cauldron of what was billed as a peaceful gathering. The movement of so many people marching as one makes my chest tighten and fills me with fear. A massive living organism is crawling through our streets and swallowing our town.

I bite down on a fingernail. My mother is out there. I search for a sign of her on the street and turn to the video feeds from our surveillance cameras.

There's no Daisy in sight. Despite all that has transpired in the last few days, I'm surprised to find I'm concerned about her safety. Wherever she is right now, I hope she's having a hell of a good time making her mark on history.

Turning to my team, I say, "We'd better get to work. Keep monitoring the camera feeds. Check the news and social media for updates. If we get a better idea of what they're planning, we'll get ahead of this."

Mimi says, "I just got a text from the security guard we placed outside the client's building. She says five teenagers with cans of spray paint are defacing the front entrance. A crowd is cheering them on."

I tap my chin. "Tell the guard not to interfere. I don't want her getting hurt by the mob. Tell her to go inside, lock the doors, and report in with updates. Brinker can hire a painter to cover it up later. Is Vincent on site?"

She says, "He is, and he was supposed to report in ten minutes ago."

I screw up my face. "He's never late to check in."

The mob roars. Thousands of united voices call out. Window panes rattle, and the building trembles. We're in the middle of a human earthquake.

I check the monitors and then glance out a window. The crowd has grown. I turn to Mimi. "What do you think? Three or four thousand people marching out there?"

She studies the feed from a camera pointing at Commercial Avenue. "More than that, I'd say."

Flora says, "Might be five thousand, crushed together."

I cross my arms. "With this many people, things can spin out of control fast. I hope the police called in reinforcements. If we stay focused on the job, we'll get through this fine."

"Roger that," Mimi says, sitting down at her desk. Her fingers fly across the key board as she brings up different websites. "I've got something," she says. "A group of protesters are meeting at city hall. Posts on socials say they want the mayor to come out and make a speech pledging support."

I roll my eyes. "Like that's going to happen."

Flora says, "Here's a post saying to rally at the shipyard and march in support of blue-collar workers. Present a united front. Manufacturing employees need to know we're behind them."

I massage my temples. "With this many people in town, they can pull off simultaneous protests in several places. But it could turn into chaos as people try to get from one area to another, and the way is blocked by a press of bodies. It's a set up for frenzied frustration, and that's when people lash out. I don't like the way this is shaping up."

Mimi says, "I don't see police officers controlling the crowd."

I glance at the computer screens. "Where are the police? Why haven't they put the barricades in place?"

Flora says, "Are we going to do anything about city hall and the shipyard?"

I shake my head. "Those two properties aren't on our docket. We'll focus our efforts on protecting our client."

Mimi points to a video feed from the client's building, where a crowd has gathered. Fists are raised. Protest signs fill the air. She says, "That doesn't look good."

My phone rings, and I see Vincent is calling.

When I answer, he says, "Sorry I'm checking in late. There's a crowd outside Bettermed's front entrance, and they're holding up signs. You might want to get down here and see it."

"I'll do that, and I'll bring Mimi along. That way, we'll be closer to the Port shed."

I hang up and say to Mimi, "We're needed at the client's offices. Things are heating up." To Flora, I say, "You're in charge while we're gone."

She brightens. "Got it, and good luck over there."

Mimi and I grab our coats, hustle outside, and head down an alley. The ground shakes from so many people marching. The air is cool. A skinny gray cat scampers in front of us and leaps on top of a green dumpster.

Across the street from Brinker's building, we come to a halt. A massive wall of writhing bodies blocks us from going further. A band plays on the stage, and people are dancing. Elbows fly, hips sway. Foreheads glisten with sweat.

"Come on," I say to Mimi. "I think we can make it through this way."

We shimmy, and shake, and snake through the masses, coming out on the other side, gasping like beached whales. Something catches my eye, and I look closer.

Three shirtless men in their twenties are climbing up the side of the Bettermed building. Bricks protrude, providing handholds. Muscles in their backs flex. Skin shines with sweat.

I pat Mimi's elbow and point. "They're heading to the roof. The air conditioning unit and mechanical systems are up there. We've got to stop them."

33

Mimi and I edge over to Bettermed's back entrance, where a security guard calls the person staffing the reception desk and tells them to let us in. The door buzzes. The lock releases. I slip inside, and Mimi follows.

Vincent meets us in the lobby. "The fact that we're not stopping people from spray painting graffiti on the building is making your mother furious. It seems she wanted a confrontation to make a show of it. She's shouting through a megaphone and insisting Brinker come out and meet with them."

My eyes open wide. "Is she crazy? We'd never allow that to happen. It's too big a security risk. Absolutely not."

Vincent clears his throat. "You may not believe this, but Brinker wants to go out there and talk with them."

My mouth falls open. "Are you sure?"

He nods.

Shaking my head, I say, "No way. We can't let him do that. We'd lose control with all those protesters out there. They could surround him and take him away and hold him as hostage until their demands are met. Given how fervent these zealots are, I bet there are no limits for them. They want to make their point to the media and the whole world."

"Agreed," Mimi and Vincent say.

Brinker comes out of a conference room and walks over to us. He's smiling, which is odd for someone whose building is being defaced. He looks tired, but his eyes are clear and bright. If I didn't know better, I'd say the activity outside his front entrance has intrigued him.

"It's quite the scene outside, isn't it?" he says. "I'll say one thing, they have passion. And I admire that." He glances through the lobby windows at a sea of people who are frowning and yelling. "I think I can calm them down. I'll explain it to them, and they'll understand."

My stomach knots. He can't take that course of action. I must prevent his folly. I inch closer to him and look him in the eyes to make my point. "I don't recommend that approach. We can't guarantee your safety if you go out there. Weren't you going to stay at home or away from work while this was going on?"

He shrugs. "It's my building, and I have a vested

interest in making sure we come through this unscathed. I'll admit, I'm also a bit curious to see first-hand what was going on. It's quite something to see all those people, isn't it? Crammed into our small town?"

"Mr. Brinker," I say. "Could I speak with you privately for a minute?"

"Sure."

As we step to the side of the lobby, a man wearing a blue security guard uniform exits the bathroom. He's got blond hair, but half of his head is shaved. On the back of his hand is a tattoo of a spider. The uniform is too tight for him. The legs of the pants are too short and end above his ankles. His red socks stand out.

I rub my lips and consider what to do. The dress code for the security guards we hired require white socks. Something is off.

Pointing to the man, I say to Brinker, "Who is that? Do you know him?"

"Sure, he's the security guard hired to cover the front door."

I release a breath. "The front door? We didn't hire him. We had a female guard posted out front. The protesters must've taken her uniform, so he could get inside."

The man disappears.

"Hold on," I say to Brinker. "I think someone got past our security guard at the front door, and he's in the building."

He frowns. I wave Vincent and Mimi over and say, "A

man came in the building off the street, and he's impersonating a security guard. He's got a spider tattoo on the back of his hand, and he just came out of the restroom."

Mimi grabs Vincent by the elbow. As they turn away, she says, "We'll handle it."

I turn to Brinker. "Sir, we have a separate issue to deal with. Three men are climbing up the side of your building. It's possible they may try to take out your mechanical system on the roof deck. We'll secure your building and haul the false security guard off the premises. I suggest you go home and stay there."

His hands fist by his sides. "It's my building, and I'm not leaving."

My pulse pounds in my ears. "Whatever you do, do not go out front. We advise you not to engage with the protesters. With an intruder inside and three men going to the roof, a third area to cover will spread us too thin. It's too risky. Please, stay inside."

He chuckles. "And look scared? That's not my style."

My eyes flicker to Mimi. "Call Flora, and tell her to get here fast. And call the police, even though they probably won't respond."

To Vincent, I say, "Find the intruder and handcuff him. I'm going up to the roof."

My gut churns. My hands clench, anticipating a fight. I step into the elevator and tap my toe with impatience on the ride up four floors.

The elevator doors open, and I step out.

The fake security guard stands there blocking my way.

In quick second, I assess him. His shoulders are slender, and he's skinny. I can take him on and win. I'll deal with him and then check the roof to stop the climbers from destroying my client's building.

I radio my team. "Found the intruder on the top floor by the door to the roof."

"On my way," Vincent replies.

I pull a zip tie from my pocket. "You're trespassing. We don't appreciate that."

The man smacks his spider tattooed fist into his palm and smiles. "I'm going to get the word out with a big, flashy scene. No one should control all the wealth and power on the planet. We're equal."

I keep him talking, so I can catch him off guard. "I agree with you."

He frowns. "I doubt that. You're part of the system, which makes you part of the problem, just like Bettermed and other tech companies are."

In a flash, I snake out my hand to grab his wrist. I twist it around, grab his other hand, and zip tie his wrists in back before he can react. I whip out another zip tie and secure him to an exposed pipe.

He howls and lunges to head butt me, but I step aside. He tries to bite me, but the bonds stop him from moving from the wall.

I tell my team over the headset, "Intruder cuffed on

the fourth floor. Come get him. I'm heading to the roof deck to deal with the wall climbers."

I go out the door to the roof deck and pull out my stun gun. Striding to the edge of the building, I peer down. One guy gave up. He's on the ground wiping his brow with his t-shirt. The two climbers have about a third of the way to go until reaching the top.

I stand at the edge and call, "Hey, you two down there. Don't come up here, or you'll be arrested. This is private property, and you're trespassing. We've called the police."

A guy with curly blond hair tips his head back and laughs. "As if the cops will arrive on a day like this. They won't get through the crowds."

His friend's face is flushed. He says, "They're probably all at the Donut House."

They both laugh.

"Very funny," I say, rolling my eyes. "How original. I'll tell you what, I'll make you an offer. If you climb down now and leave the property, we won't arrest you."

The blond guy says, "We can't. We made a bet, and I don't like to lose. And we're getting paid for this stunt. All we have to do now is..."

His friend cuts him off. "Don't tell. We promised we wouldn't say what we're supposed to do. Keep your mouth shut."

I put my hands on my hips and say, "How much are you getting paid for this?"

"Fifty bucks each," the blond says.

"Listen, I'll double that. All I ask is that you go down immediately and collect your money at the back entrance. Why not? It's easy, and you won't have to fight me up here. I can guarantee you won't win. Not only that, I've got friends who are on their way."

"What'd think, Biff?" the blond says.

"I like the idea, but how do we know she's telling the truth? She might arrest us as soon as we reach the ground."

"I give you my word," I say. "We won't arrest you if you go down now."

A whispered discussion ensues.

The blond says, "Okay, we accept your offer. See you by the back door."

I wait a moment to make sure they're climbing down and not tricking me.

I radio my team, "The climbers are on their way down. I promised them money if they descend and don't cause trouble."

When the climbers on the sidewalk, I say into my headset, "The climbers are off the building and down on the ground. Give the rosy-cheeked man and a curly-haired blond one hundred dollars each."

Mimi says, "Roger that. When you can, take a look up there from the west side of the building. Your mother is making a scene. Thought you'd want to know."

I cringe. If only Daisy would get out of my hair and

stop causing me extra work. I can't wait until she leaves town. I don't think I ever want to speak with her again.

"Right," I say. "I'll do that. Did you pick up the man impersonating a security guard on the fourth floor?"

Vincent says, "I checked, but he wasn't there. He must've managed to uncuff his wrists."

I smack my forehead. "He's loose in the building, and we have no idea where he is?"

Mimi says, "We're going floor by floor right now, looking for him. He'll turn up."

My jaw clenches. "We need to nab him before he does too much damage."

Vincent says in a tight voice, "The client just went outside. I repeat, Brinker is out front. He said he wants to reason with the protesters."

"I'll head over there now," I say.

I take a quick look over the roof as Mimi advised. Down below, Daisy is jabbing a finger at my client's chest. He's waving his arms. The situation is escalating, but it's not because of my failures. My client refused to listen to reason or advice from trained professionals.

When I turn to go to the elevator, a man slips his forearm around my neck.

I gasp and try to take his legs out from under him while knocking his arm away.

Standing behind me, he tightens his grip and yanks hard, choking me. The bone in his arm cuts off my air.

I cough, issuing a strangled sound. Tears fill my eyes.

Adrenaline surges through my veins as I scrabble at the air, searching for flesh.

"You're not going anywhere," he says. "This is for locking me up."

34

———

I use my fingers as weapons and aim for his eyes. The fake security guard keeps hold of me and shakes me from side to side.

He speaks into my ear in a low voice, "So you're Daisy's daughter? I was at your place last night with your mom. You act all high and mighty. They say too much pride comes before a fall."

Hairs in my ears prickle. His lips brush against my ear lobe. His breath is warm.

I splutter and stomp down on his feet.

He swears but keeps a hold of me, choking me.

Gasping for air, I shove a hand in my jacket pocket for my stun gun. I don't want to use the pistol unless I'm forced to. In this close proximity, if I pull it out, he might grab it and use it against me.

I'm about to flip him over when he whips my body around. "Not today, sunshine."

He drags me toward the edge of the roof, but I claw at his eyes.

He yelps.

I break from his grasp and turn around, kicking him in the knees. When my boot heel smashes his knee cap, he collapses with a groan.

I pull out my stun gun and step back, aiming at him. I could use the pistol in my holster, but the stun gun will do the job and involve less paperwork.

Vincent bursts out onto the roof and runs over. "We wondered why you were taking so long. What happened?"

"He attacked me. I think he was going to throw me off the roof."

The fake guard holds up his hands. "Hold on, I didn't do anything. I'm innocent."

"Stay there," I say. "And don't move."

He issues a theatrical sigh, and his arms go limp by his sides, as if he's giving up. But he's a sly one. I don't believe his act.

I say to Vincent, "Let's handcuff him and lock him in the janitor's closet. We'll deal with him later. The police never came when you called, did they?"

"No cops," says the fake guard with the half-shaved head. Sweat drips down his forehead. "Please, I'll do whatever you say. I just want to go out and join Daisy in the protest."

I give Vincent a look. What is it about my mom that makes people want to follow her so much? Maybe I missed how mesmerizing she could be when I was growing up, because we lived in close proximity. Our house held the resentments and longings we harbored as two women who had been left behind for someone new and better.

I wanted to live with my dad and my biological mother. Daisy wanted my father to ditch his younger mistress, come back to her and for him to kick me out of the house. Neither of us got what we wanted.

Vincent says, "The police haven't shown up. They're busy at the moment. The dispatcher said they're flooded with calls, and it'll take a while. They might not even get to us until tomorrow."

I say, "Waiting with this guy until tomorrow is like a year in another reality. We can't wait for them to appear. You flip him over and cuff him. I'll aim the gun at him."

I aim the stun gun while Vincent flips the guy over and zip ties his wrists.

I say, "Add a second one. Use two for extra measure. He got away once."

Vincent hauls the man to his feet and says, "You've got an important date with a dark closet. We might let you out later, when we have time to deal with you."

The man hawks up saliva and spits at me. A glob of sputum splats on my cheek, sliding down.

With a sneer, I wipe the moist mess off with the back

of my hand and wipe it on my pants. "March to the eleva-tor. Now."

Vincent pushes him ahead. I join them on the elevator and push the button for the lobby. On the elevator ride down, I say, "Where is the female guard who was posted at the front entrance?"

The fake guard presses his lips together and is silent.

Vincent shakes his shoulders. "What did you do with the guard? Where is she?"

He smiles. "I'm not telling."

This guy strikes me as an off the beam type motivated by an inner calling. I don't think Daisy would have sent him to harm me. But a thought occurs to me. I can see Daisy wanting to hurt Bettermed and wreck their equip-ment. It would fit with her crusade of taking back power from big companies to help the everyday person.

I say to Vincent, "Did you check each office in the building to make sure he didn't damage something? What about the server room?"

Vincent is about to answer when the fake guard says with a grin, "I took a dump on Brinker's desk. That's a statement. I showed him. I was going to hit the server room, but you caught me first."

I grind my teeth and glance at Vincent, who shakes his head. No need to engage with this creep. We're above smacking him for his uncouth behavior. I want to hit him, but I won't. We'll call a cleaning crew in and wipe it from our minds.

We march him down the hall and shove him in a closet. I'm about to close the door when it occurs to me that because he got out of the cuffs once, he could do it again. The closet holds all kinds of things that could be used as a weapon, like a broom.

I nudge Vincent. "Hold on. I think we're making a mistake."

"Yeah," the man with the half-shaved head says.

I say, "The police won't be here for hours, maybe not until tomorrow. And this guy is like Houdini. He could get out again. We don't have time to haul him to the police station. It would take forever to get through the crowd."

Vincent's eyes light up. "What if we perp walked him out front and exchanged him for Brinker? Things are getting heated out there. Your mother has our client surrounded, and she won't let him leave."

I rub a finger across my lips and consider his idea. "That could work. Let's try it."

We pull the man from the closet and push him through the lobby.

He says, "You can't prove I did anything wrong."

Vincent and I exchange a look.

I say, "Whatever you do, don't come back to this building ever again. If we see you on site, even on the sidewalk, we'll come for you."

He sniffs. "Understood."

We push the front door open and propel the fake security guard outside. Sniffing the air, I smell smoke. The jewelry store's tall round clock across the street shows the time is almost noon.

Daisy yells to the crowd through her recently acquired appendage, a megaphone.

Brinker stands by her side, and he's listening.

I go up and tap my mom on the shoulder.

When she turns and sees me, her mouth falls open.

"What are you doing here?" she says. "You'd better leave. This is my event."

Brinker nods to me. He smiles, as if his being here wasn't the worst idea on the planet. He seems oddly interested in the proceedings.

Vincent brings the fake guard over to stand by Brinker.

The crowd boos.

A man in a knit cap calls out, "Look, there's a guard! Let's get him!"

A woman in a red beret says with a gravelly voice, "He's one of us. Don't hurt him."

But it's too late. The crowd is on the move, and no one pays attention to what she said. Shoving ensues as the crowd surges forward. A fist fight breaks out between two middle-aged men in jeans with beer bellies.

"Stop!" Daisy yells. "Step back. Don't rush the front."

People press ahead. An older woman cries out in pain.

A child whimpers. A baby screams. A man barks, "Don't push."

Before we're pressed in a crush of bodies, I reach out and grab Brinker's arm.

"Sir, we need to get out of here. Let's go."

Just then, police whistles blow. People panic and try to run. Officers rap clubs against their clear plastic shields.

The cops close in, and the crowd tries to flee. Protesters use signs as weapons. They poke and prod and jab. They whack helmeted heads.

The police move in carrying barricades. A line of officers in blue close in on the mob. The scrum of people knots.

An officer pepper sprays a teenage girl. She screams, drops her protest sign, and runs. Shouts pierce the air.

An older man in a red beanie is pepper sprayed, and he tries to hit the cop. The officer whacks him on the shoulder with a club. He crumples to the pavement and cries out. On his knees, he closes his eyes and yells, "My eyes are burning. Help me."

Protesters scream and run.

A middle-aged woman with a blue bandana on her head pulls a small child along by the hand. The boy wails and plants his feet in the road. People push past. The woman bends and scoops the kid up in her arms before running off.

The cloud of pepper spray grows, making my eyes smart.

The crowd turns as one and runs down the street, heading toward the Port shed building on Cedar Channel.

I frown. The protesters will be boxed in and right by the Port shed. If the shed is set ablaze, the group will panic. There could be casualties from a stampede or the fire.

I place my body in front of Brinker, who is pressed against a wall, and shield him from harm.

35

———

With a loud whomp, the wooden Port building bursts into flames. Thick smoke fills the air. Brinker and I cough. Clumps of people claw their way in the opposite direction, but they're blocked by the sheer masses of bodies. There are too many of them to pivot and turn with ease. The police press on, seemingly oblivious or awaiting fresh orders.

Sirens pierce the air, coming closer.

People shriek.

When the sirens stop, I wonder if they can get through the mass of protesters, or past the RVs and trucks parked in side streets. I suspect the fire trucks don't have a way to get through, and we don't have time to wait for tow trucks to clear the lanes.

Ashes land on people's shoulders and in our hair. It

looks like it's snowing, and it stinks of acrid smoke. Smoke billows. I blink and wipe my watering eyes.

"Come on," I say to my client. "Let's get you indoors and out of this mess."

Vincent and I guide him inside. We lock the doors and close the lobby blinds.

Brinker wipes his face with a handkerchief and says with a smile, "What a firebrand your mother is. It's rare for someone to try to put me in my place."

I cock my head. This day is getting weirder and weirder.

He says, "She's an exceptional leader. I admire that quality in a person." He rubs his cheek.

I scratch my head. He's certainly changed after his exposure to the protest mob. Who would have thought? I guess I don't know him that well or Daisy after all.

I say, "Back to business, sir, would it be all right if we went to your office and monitored the fire? I'm worried it might make its way here and burn your building."

His face flushes. "Of course, right this way."

As we go to his office, Vincent takes me aside. "Did you forget about the gift that guy left on the client's desk?"

I wince. "Damn it, I did forget. We'd better hurry and take care of it before Mr. B. sees it."

Despite hurrying ahead, the three of us arrive at the door to Brinker's office at the same time. A woman on the cleaning crew comes out right then, waving a hand in front of her nose. She has long black hair and prominent cheekbones. She's wearing an apron.

She wrinkles her nose and pulls off her disposable gloves. "Some people are disgusting. What that man did, I'll never understand."

Brinker says, "Morgana, you weren't supposed to come in today. I told you to take the day off."

She nods. "I know, but given the hubbub in town, I thought a clean office would help keep you calm despite what's going on. I read about the trouble in the papers and came down to do my part to help."

"Thank you," Brinker says. "This is much appreciated. Now go home and take the rest of the day off with pay."

I murmur to Vincent, "Guess we dodged a brown bullet. She took care of it. Thank goodness."

The office smells like Morgana was liberal in spraying air freshener, but that's better than opening the windows and letting in thick smoke tinged with pepper spray. We stand at the windows overlooking Cedar Channel and watch the Port shed burn. Orange and black flames shoot up, leaping higher.

A fireboat in the channel blasts water at the burning building on the waterfront. A second fireboat joins in the effort. Twin sprays from huge nozzles hit the fire, but it rages on. A rainbow appears in the mist created by the fire hoses.

I tap the window glass with my index finger. "Look. Over there. A rainbow."

Brinker says, "Beauty amid chaos. What a day this has been. What a few days, in fact."

Vincent and I nod.

I say, "Indeed. We could say it was most unexpected. But from the threat you received and the social media postings, I think we knew it might be a blow out."

Brinker says, "If only the police had thought so too. There was so much they could've done to prepare. They should've called in reinforcements earlier."

Vincent says, "And not pepper sprayed little old ladies coming out of hair salons."

"Definitely," Brinker says. "I'll have you know, that was my mother. Her eyes are still hurting. It was traumatic for her, to say the least."

I give him a close look as he wipes his eyes. "I had no idea."

Brinker's jaw is set as he looks out on the fire. "I'll do everything in my power to make sure the chief of police steps down after this. Businesses should have no confidence in him. He mismanaged this event."

I say, "I agree, but might've been a mess anyway, even if he was more prepared."

My client shakes his head. "That's no excuse for what happened here."

"Oh, look," Vincent says.

We spin around just as the Port shed falls in on itself and collapses. The three of us let out a collective gasp. The building we're in trembles and then falls quiet. A cloud of dust and black smoke rises and hovers for a moment before blowing away.

On the street, in a haze of dirty air, people are fleeing the fire. Orders for the police officers must have changed. They're marching in a line and pushing the crowd south on Commercial now, away from the channel and the fire.

A woman in an orange caftan catches my eye.

"There's Daisy," I say.

A cop raises a club and strikes her on the back. I bite my lip. That would hurt.

When the officer points south, she puts her hands to her face and runs down the street, followed by others.

Brinker blurts out, "She was clubbed by an officer. If I was down there, I'd get his badge number." He frowns and turns toward the door. "I've got to do something. I can't just stand here and let people get hurt."

I move to block his way and put my hands out. "Sir, this is a time to stand down and let the situation work itself out. Adding one more body to the mix out there won't calm the waters. You'd be just one of the people scurrying for safety like my mother is."

He sighs and sinks into a chair. Leaning forward and running his hands through his thick silver hair, he says, "If only we hadn't held the trade association talks in Millersville. Our town would've remained calm. A tranquil haven for what ails you, guaranteed to bring down your blood pressure." He looks up at me. "That's why people move here, including me."

I say, "You had no way to know the talks would ignite a mob. Or that anarchists would come and roam the streets, breaking windows." He doesn't look convinced, so I add, "Just think about Seattle's WTO meeting in 1999 and what happened there. Do you remember the Battle in Seattle?"

Vincent says, "I've heard of it. But it was back in the day."

Brinker shrugs. "I didn't pay much attention to it. I was busy running a company, expanding sales and making a better product. Next time someone brings up a bright idea of holding talks here, I'll shut them down. No need to damage paradise any further."

My phone buzzes with a text, and I pull it out of my pocket.

Mimi says, "The police chief called out the National Guard, but it was too late. Everyone is blaming him on social media. They're not so fond of the mayor either."

I relay the information to Brinker, who shakes his head.

"What a shame," he says. "I had civic pride, but now it's tarnished. I'll do all I can to vote the mayor out in the next election."

I swallow hard, feeling like a traitor for what I'm about to say. "I consider her to be a friend, but I share your feelings."

Brinker says, "And the chief of police, what was he thinking?"

I shrug. "I'm not sure. He was warned ahead of time, but he waved it off as no big deal."

Brinker scratches his day-old beard. "None of us want to be seen as a fool if we prepare for battle and nothing happens. But he clearly made the wrong call." He glances at Vincent and me and wags a finger at us. "This conversation is just between us, understood?"

"Absolutely, sir," I say. "It'll go no further."

Vincent and I say goodbye and walk outside. Someone pushed the porta potties over on their sides. I wrinkle my nose and breathe through my mouth.

Vincent chuckles. "Welcome to Millersville. The home of the riots. What a mess."

I say, "We did everything we could for our client. I'm proud of our team."

A young woman sits on the curb in tattered clothes. She rubs her eyes, and she's crying. I take a close look at her and start.

I say to Vincent, "Doesn't that look like the missing security guard we posted at the front entrance?"

"I believe so. Let's go talk to her. See if we can help."

I sit down next to her. "Are you okay? You look pretty upset."

She says, "I didn't guard the building well enough. They took my uniform and made me wear this instead. I think I just lost my job."

I pat her on the shoulder. "That was an angry mob. It was too much for one person to handle. My company hired you, and I don't want you to worry about it. Just take care of yourself."

She sniffs and studies me. "Really?"

"Yeah, I mean it. Do you want to come to the office with us and get cleaned up?"

She lets out a long sigh. "Sure. I didn't count on it getting violent. I thought it'd be an easy gig, sitting at a desk and checking people's ID. I need to get another job."

I nod. "I understand. Not everyone is cut out for a job like this."

"I'll second that," Vincent says.

36

———

The security guard in tattered clothes and I stand. I brush myself off as Vincent waits for us. Ashes from the fire are falling and irritating my eyes.

Five people run past at a fast clip. They're yelling and screaming with arms outstretched, as if escaping something horrible.

A balding man in his sixties rips off a turtle costume and throws it on the pavement. He walks off with his head down, looking dejected.

A woman in her twenties stops near us and sobs. "They're spraying tear gas." Her t-shirt is smeared with dirt. Her jeans are ripped at the knees and thighs, but they may have already been that way to be fashionable. She bends over and pants, resting her hands on her knees.

A man about her age wearing a poncho, jeans, and flip flops pats her on the shoulder. He says to me, "They're using rubber bullets and concussion grenades on us."

My eyebrows shoot up. I didn't expect that. Talk about going from zero to sixty in seconds flat. If they'd taken measures earlier to control the situation, we might have avoided this mayhem.

The female protester's eyes are red and watering. She says, "They're ordering us to disperse. But we're peaceful protesters. We're not the anarchists wrecking things to make a statement."

I pull a water bottle I took from a tray in Brinker's office out of my pocket and offer it to the couple. "Here, you can have this. Be careful. Get to safety as soon as you can."

She takes the water and tugs at her stained white shirt. Glancing at the security guard who is standing with us, she says, "Whatever happened to us, it doesn't look as bad as what hit you. Take care of yourselves. Be strong in solidarity."

The two run off, holding hands.

"We need a plan," I say, "for how to get back to the office, given the rubber bullets, tear gas, and stun grenades. We can't go down Commercial, where the battle is raging. I don't want us getting caught up in it."

The security guard crosses her arms. "I agree with that."

Vincent says, "We can skirt the skirmishes by running

down side streets. It's only three blocks. We'll be fine."

The security guard trembles. "I hope so," she says.

I point at Vincent. "You go first, and we'll follow behind. I'll take up the rear position. Let's stick together and get back to the office. Let's go."

We snake down a side street, keeping close to buildings. We're running and staying low. My shoulders ache from hunching over and from the tension of today's events. My throat is dry. But that doesn't matter now. We need to get into the office and shut the door and help the guard who is with us. When I look at her, I see terror in her eyes.

"Just a little longer," I say to her. "Hang on."

Stragglers from the broken-up crowd hurry past the marina and stream down R Avenue, heading south to their cars and transportation. On Commercial, a block away, protesters scream. I grimace. Remnants of tear gas drift our way. We close our eyes and cough, making hacking sounds.

I squint through my smarting eyes and glance toward the melee. Protesters are raising their fists and yelling at police. Officers dressed in riot gear with helmets and shields are shoving screaming protesters down the street. A woman trips and falls. Others stumble into her.

Angry shouts fill the air. At the crack of a gun, people scream. Shot ring out with a resounding boom. Protesters run screaming from the rubber bullets.

Moving on, we approach our street. Vincent goes

ahead and looks around the corner. He motions for us to follow. As I bring up the rear, I wonder how something like this could happen here in tourist town U.S.A.

"Not much further now," I tell the security guard.

She nods.

We creep down the side street. We're only two store fronts away from the office when a concussion grenade goes off with a blinding flash of light and an intense bang.

My ears ring. My eyes hurt. A splitting headache throbs.

We're in the midst of a battle. Before this week, the biggest problems we had in town were the growing wild deer population grazing on roses and catalytic converter thefts. Local residents had no idea what trouble was until now.

I reach out and put a hand on the door to the building where Outrigger Services rents space. We're almost there. Safety is close at hand.

I hold the door open and wait while Vincent ushers the security guard inside. With a last look at the chaos raging outside, I step into the lobby and wonder if the town can survive this event and emerge intact. I'm not sure we'll ever be the same. I know Daisy and I won't.

"Let's take the stairs," I say.

As we charge up the stairs to the office, I think of Daisy being vulnerable out there on the streets. As far as I know, she doesn't have a gas mask. She's unprotected from tear gas, pepper spray, rubber bullets, and stun grenades. Even though I'm ticked off at her for breaking into my home, I don't want to see her injured.

37

We burst into the Outrigger offices. Flora and Mimi look up at us with wide eyes. They drop what they're doing and stand. I'm panting after running up the stairs, and my heart is racing after running from the scene on the street.

I close the office door and lean back against it.

I say, "We need to get this guard a shower, some food, and fresh clothes. Does anyone have sweat pants and a shirt they can give her? We need to debrief after we get her settled."

Mimi raises her hand. "I do. Come with me."

"Great."

They disappear down a hall, and I collapse in Mimi's chair.

Vincent slumps in his seat.

Flora says, "What happened to you guys? We were worried about you."

I blow out a breath. "It's ugly out there. I'm glad we made it back."

The sound of breaking glass brings us to the windows.

Down below, anarchists in black run down the street smashing windows.

I let out a low whistle. "By the time they're through, there won't be a sheet of glass in downtown on street level they haven't blown out."

The sound of pounding footsteps coming up the stairwell makes me glance at Vincent.

I say," Let's secure the premises in case someone tries to break in and wreck the place."

We lock the door and pull out our weapons, aiming at the entrance.

The door knob turns. Someone pushes on it with a thud. When it doesn't open, they smack it with their fists. The door shakes.

My pulse pounds in my ears. Who could it be? What if the anarchists break in and smash the equipment I just bought?

I keep my arm steady and aim at the door.

"Flora," I say, "who is it? Can you see who it is from the security camera?"

"It's a woman and a man. I can't make out much. They're standing in front of the camera."

A body thumps against the door. The knob turns and rattles. Someone really wants to get inside.

I frown. We installed the camera after I signed the lease. I didn't count on not being able to see clearly if a threat is at our threshold.

"Let me in," a woman says. It sounds like Daisy's voice. "We need help."

"I think that's my mom," I say.

Vincent furrows his brow. "Can we trust her?"

I furrow my brow. "I'm not sure."

My mom says, "Help! Violet, let me in."

I release a breath and lower my arm, holstering my gun. I hope what I'm about to do won't jeopardize the safety of my team or the reputation of my new company.

Going up to the door and speaking through it, I say, "What's wrong? Why are you here?"

Daisy says, "Ralph took some rubber bullets on his belly. He's hurting and needs medical attention. We breathed tear gas. We need to wash our eyes out with water, and we can't find any. You've got to help us."

I say, "Is anyone with you?"

I don't want a horde of people coming in here and damaging the office on purpose. They could trash the place and make a video of it, crowing about it on social media. What if she brough the anarchists with her? I cringe. It's not beyond possibility.

"No, it's just us," she says. "No one else is here."

As I turn to Flora and Vincent to say something, Mimi and the guard join us.

"What's going on?" Mimi says, frowning. "Who is at the door? Why is it locked?"

"Daisy is out there. She wants to come in for first aid for her and her friend." I look at my team. "Are you okay with my letting them in? I'm inclined to do so, but I'm biased. I realize it is a risk. It's possible this is a ruse, and they'll try something."

Mimi says, "We've been on opposite sides. So, it's odd they'd come to us. It's almost suspicious."

"But she is your family member," Flora says.

Vincent nods. "We saw what it was like out there. They may be sincere in seeking shelter. I vote we let them in. Everyone agreed?"

"Yes," Mimi and Flora say.

The security guard is silent. She tugs on a strand of wet hair. Her hands tremble.

I point to the guard. "You, wait in the kitchen. See if you can find something to eat. Stay out of the way because we're not entirely sure about the people we're letting in."

She turns in her yellow sweatpants and sweatshirt and scurries off.

I point to Vincent. "Just in case, keep a gun trained on them. I don't trust them. But if they're truly hurt, we need to help them."

Mimi unlocks the door and opens it.

My mom barges in. Her friend Ralph hobbles in after her.

I hold up a hand. "Stop right there. Before we let you in, do you agree to behave yourselves?"

Daisy sobs. Her face is blotchy. Her eyes are swollen and red.

"Yes, just let us in. We need help."

38

I usher Daisy into the kitchen area, and Ralph, the protester leader, shuffles behind. Our security guard is sitting at the table. She swallows a bite of a granola bar and breaks into a coughing fit. She squirms in her seat, as if she'd rather not share the small room with two protesters who may be connected to her capture.

I hand Daisy a water bottle. "Rinse your eyes with this at the sink."

I give one to Ralph, and he nods. His face is pale and lined with wrinkles. He looks about ten years older than when I first spotted him in the planning meeting. But that was eons ago in Millersville protest time.

When they finish pouring water into their eyes and splashing tap water on their faces, I hand them paper towels. Vincent lurks at the doorway with his weapon ready, just in case they try a last-minute insurrection and make a stand at our polar-opposite position offices.

My mom says, "It's rough out there. Worse than at any protest I've attended. How about you, Ralph?"

"Same. I somehow didn't expect the concussion grenades or plastic bullets. I'd heard they only had a few police officers on the force, and I assumed it'd be an easy takeover of the town."

Our guard's jaw is tight with tension.

I say to her, "If you want, you can go in the bullpen. Talk to Mimi about what to do next."

She gives me a grateful nod and gets up, leaving the room.

"Glad she left," Daisy says. "I didn't like the looks of her when she was guarding the entrance to your client's building. If someone looks afraid, it attracts the attention of angry people. A fearful guard riles them up to deliver what's expected, which is violence."

I study her face. I didn't realize my mom knew about the psychology of warfare. Don't show fear or your opposition can smell it. Stand your ground with confidence and own your turf.

"But," my mom says, "it's a shame when violence happens to someone that meek. I told the fringe element who did this not to make her switch clothes. The poor kid."

"I should hope so," I say, drumming my fingers on the table. "She's pretty traumatized by it, and I can see why. By the way, the guy with the half-shaved head who put on her guard uniform attacked me. He tried to throw me off the roof."

She reaches over and squeezes my hand. "He's a loose cannon. We've tried to control him. You always have an outlier in any group."

I jerk my hand away from her, appalled at how she doesn't care that I almost died.

Ralph rubs his flushed forehead. "We've tried to oust him, but he keeps coming back. I just hope he doesn't bring a gun with him next time."

I flinch, picturing the man in question wielding a firearm. The word danger is an understatement. A shiver runs up my spine, and I shudder.

"You need to report him to the police. He's a menace and a ticking time bomb then. What about the anarchists? Are they aligned with you and your cause?"

My mom pounds on the table with a fist. "No, they're not. I'm ticked they came here and disrupted our peaceful protest. They popped up out of nowhere and took advantage of the protest we arranged. Talk about ruining our reputation."

Ralph picks at a cuticle. "I've spoken to the guy who said he was their leader. They aren't aligned with any organization. They wanted media coverage, that's all. And they're not going to stop."

My mom says, "Do you have any food? I'm hungry. It's been ages since breakfast at the RV park."

I open the cupboards and haul out some snack bars and take a few green apples from a red ceramic bowl on the counter. I hand the fruit to them. They deserve sour apples for what they did to my house, and we can gather intel from them.

Going to the doorway, I say, "Mimi, I could use your help in here. Bring a notepad. You may want to take notes. Vincent, you're welcome to join us. You can holster your weapon now. I don't think they came here to harm us."

When we're gathered around the table, I say, "We've all been through a lot in the last few days. It would help if we knew more about the anarchists and any other splinter groups, like the people who started the fire at the port shed."

Mimi pulls out a pen and positions her hand over a lined notepad.

My mom turns to Ralph. "Should we tell them?"

He shrugs. "As long as we don't tell secrets or mention members, I think we'll be fine. They're offering us shelter now, after all."

Daisy scratches the corner of her mouth. She does that when she's deep in thought. She says, "All I know about the splinter groups is what I found on chat rooms, message boards, and the internet. Probably just like you're tracking."

I nod and stay silent, using a negotiation technique.

Ralph is the one who speaks up. "We know the anarchists came from Eugene, Oregon. They're a tight group and not easy to infiltrate. They're different from us. We're in it to educate everyday people and policy makers. They like to grab attention by breaking things."

My mom chimes in. "The anarchists are an unknown. We're not sure what motivates them. But we don't like them piggybacking on our event. People reading the news might assume we're all here to smash windows and loot local stores."

I make a note to keep tabs on the group from Eugene, which is five or six hours south of Millersville.

I say, "And the fire at the port shed? Do you know who started that?"

She glances at Ralph. "We didn't authorize that action. I'm not sure who did that. It might've been some pyromaniacs or college students."

Ralph steeples his hands and rests them on the table. "We're non-violent. We don't encourage breaking into buildings or setting fires. We believe we can change consumers' minds about what to buy and how to live without resorting to arson or breaking and entering."

I give Daisy a long, hard look and say, at the risk of their refusing to share more information, "Really? Is that right?"

They both nod.

My heart pounds. I stare at them, and my hands fist in my lap. "What about my home? You broke in there. Why was that an exception?"

Daisy clears her throat.

Ralph coughs and covers his mouth.

I let the silence in the room speak for itself. A few seconds later, I say, "Nice of you, Daisy, to make an exception for your daughter by ruining my place."

She waves a hand in front of her nose. Perspiration beads on her brow. "I wouldn't say it was exactly like that. It was more of a spur of the moment, as needed decision. We were hungry and thirsty. And I needed to take a long shower."

I scowl. It all comes back to what Daisy wants. "Remember this," I say, tapping a trimmed fingernail on the table. "Next time you're in town, if that ever happens, avoid my home. Stay fifty feet away from it, or I'll report you to the police for trespassing. There will be no repeats of what happened. You're not welcome back."

I pound a fist on the table to make it clear I'm done with their two-faced lies and self-interested actions. "If anything," I say, and my throat closes with tears, "you should've been more considerate of me because I'm your daughter. You shouldn't have taken advantage of me and our relationship. I won't be your doormat in the future. I expect you to adhere to the law, especially when around me, because that's my business."

Daisy says, "Well, aren't you a sensitive one these days. You're still like you were when you were a teenager, aren't you? We only opened the window that time, and the back door last night. You should let it go. Think of the joy you brought others."

I clench my teeth. There's no joy in Millersville with Daisy around. My muscles ache. My neck hurts if I look to the left. My right eye twitches. I am so tired. I can't wait to get a decent night's sleep in my own bed.

I stand and say, "We'll show you to the showers. That's a popular spot today."

My mom gets up. She touches her chin, like she does when she's uneasy. "Don't tell anyone we talked to you. We never spoke. And thank you for letting us in and giving us shelter when we needed it." She stares at me and says, "Just like the other afternoon and last night when we were camped out."

I suppress a groan. Daisy isn't growing wiser about her impact on my life, despite my efforts to provide feedback. It might be best if I gave up and cut her off. It's sad because she's an important part of my past.

"Come on," I say, motioning for Daisy and Ralph to follow me. "I'll take you to the shower area."

As we amble down the hall, I hope my staff won't bring up what Daisy said at the table. My pretense of not caring about my childhood and my family evaporated when I spoke to my mom about how hurt I felt. My personal hell arrived this week because of what Daisy said and did.

Thanks a million, Mom. Happy Protesters' Week. You know how to ruin my calm and peaceful life.

39

We usher my mom and her friend to the door an hour later. My mom snakes out an arm and snags me in a hug, even though I resist. She says, "You act like you're all big and grown, but I know how much you like a hug."

Muffled in her embrace, I roll my eyes to my staff. I'm reduced to being eleven years old in her arms.

When I step away, she says, "You're looking good, and I'm proud of you, Vi."

She studies the office. "It's remarkable really. You're in charge of all this." She turns to my team, who are standing in a half circle with their hands in the fig leaf position.

Daisy says, "She's a special one. Take care of her." She gazes at me. "You are the sweetest daughter I could ever have, and I'm glad you came into my life."

I swallow and tears come to my eyes. This is what I've wanted to hear since the day I had to move in with her.

She says to my crew, "When she was young, I'd march for causes, while she was home studying or cleaning the kitchen or running."

She pauses and tilts her head. I hope she's finished with her intimate reveal and ultimate humiliation in front of my employees.

But she continues. "You were always running, isn't that right? Do you all run too? She loves to do that, pounding on pavement and racing up hills."

Mimi smiles. "Sure, a bunch of us go out at lunchtime and tear up the Tommy Thompson trial."

Daisy puts a hand on the door knob. "I don't understand the urge to always be in motion, but I respect the drive you all have. We're on separate sides, but we can still respect each other, can't we?"

My crew and I stand silently.

I drop my hands to my sides. I want Daisy to her leave and stop giving out private nuggets from my past. I reach past her and open the door. "See you around, Daisy."

She lands a kiss on my cheek. "See you around, sweet girl."

Ralph follows her out, and I lock the door. I wonder if what just transpired left a shred of esteem for me in my team's minds.

Tapping my lips, I suppose if it's possible to be a leader and a daughter to Daisy at the same time. I like to keep my personal and professional lives separate, but Daisy just blew the hatch off that practice.

I say, "That was a rare look at my family life. Let's get back to our debriefing."

We sit around exchanging views, discussing what worked and what didn't in how we handled the mission of protecting our client's company. Despite my worries, my staff acts like my mother's revelations never wafted through the office, and their respect for me remains intact.

"That's enough for today," I say, standing up. "Anyone who wants to join me, the first round is on me at the Brown Lantern. If it's open after the rioting, that is."

The traumatized security guard leans against the window sill. She asked to listen, and we let her sit in and observe.

"You're welcome to come," I say to her. "I'm sorry, but I forget. What was your name?"

"Polly," she says. "This was interesting. If you ever have a job opening, I'd like to work here."

Mimi says, "We'll keep it in mind. Hey, boss, your mom was certainly interesting." She grins at me. "Quite the social life when you were a teenager, huh? Cleaning the kitchen while your mom was out on the warpath?"

I poke her in the shoulder and smile. "You don't want to hear how exciting that was."

But the truth is, the biggest excitement I had in those days was going upstairs and sneaking into the off-limits attic. With every footstep going up the pull-down steps, my heart thumped. I wasn't supposed to go up there. That much I knew.

My mind flits back to the past. I asked my dad when I was young, "Why can't I go up there? You do. Why can't I?"

My dad stared at his shoes, which was uncharacteristic of him. "It isn't safe. You might fall off the steps. Nothing's up there but dusty old papers and old furniture."

Somehow though, from the way his eyes shifted when he talked about the attic, it made me want to climb up there all the more. I wanted to find out if they were hiding anything of value or interest above where I slept.

"Ready?" Vincent says, bringing me back to the present. "The Brown is our next stop. I doubt it's open after the disaster this afternoon. If it isn't, I'll head straight home."

I say, "You can do that. We'd understand."

"No," he says, "I don't want to miss this celebration. We've been through a battle and came out the other side."

I grab my wallet, shrug into my coat, and we're out the door.

On the street, shirts, hats, and protest signs are abandoned. Water bottles roll back and forth on the pavement in a slight breeze. Rain clouds have scuttled off, bringing blue skies and a smell of salt air coming off Cedar Channel.

The screaming has moved to a distant part of town. Yelling from fewer voices hums like bees in the background. The threat has moved on.

The lights at the Brown Lantern are on, and the green door opens.

"Hey," I say to my crew, "we're in luck."

We walk in the bar, and a hush falls over the room. I glance around. The atmosphere is charged. Did we enter a lion's den of patrons who secretly despise security services and those tangential to law enforcement?

Ignoring the stares, I say to Mimi, "Grab a table. I'll get the drinks."

I belly up to a polished wood bar. After the week we've had, nothing will stop me from enjoying a glass of beer with people I respect and admire.

Conversations around me pick up again. The irritation, if there was any, has passed, and the rancor subsided. We're safe here, for now at least.

I scan the room. The tables are full. A gray-haired grizzled man in his seventies waves to my group and stands.

"You can have our table." He gestures to his friends who are around the same age. "We appreciate what you did by protecting Mr. Brinker's building. We'll go out to the beer garden while I wait for my food order."

"Thanks. It's kind of you." I lean on the bar, and my shoulders relax. It feels good to be recognized and appreciated for our efforts.

As he and his buddies file out, my staff slides into seats around a scarred round table.

The bartender comes over to me and says, "What'll it be?"

Bets the bartender has a ready smile and a small black mole on the right side of her nose. She's wearing designer glasses with white frames. She tends bar here with her husband, Zerk. They're the life of the party, even on dull Mondays, and I admire how they embrace life and laugh together.

I smile at her and get the sense once again, for the umpteenth time, that she and Zerk have been on many roads before landing here in our little town. Places they won't talk about, and that's fine. We all carry secrets from the past.

I order a round of drinks for my crew. We've worked together long enough that I knew their preferences. Then I remember Polly has joined us.

I call over to her. "What'll it be, Polly?"

Bets chortles. "That rhymes. What'll it be Poll-ee?" She repeats it and breaks into a fit of giggles.

Pretty soon, my team and I are saying the phrase and chuckling. We've been through the washing cycle in the last few days and come out slap happy. We're laughing to relieve tension, because it's not that funny.

Glancing around the wood paneled room, I let out a contented sigh. It's good to be around folks who aren't screaming or beating on a drum for a cause. I've had enough of zealots, including Daisy. I need a break.

"What a week, eh?" I say to Bets as Polly gets up to join me.

Bets lets out a low whistle. "Mayhem and madness is

what it was. We were packed. No sissy drinks were served. It was all beer and whiskey for the protesters, with an occasional I'll just take a water, please. Our regulars had a hard time finding seats."

Polly steps up to the bar and orders a negroni.

Bets flashes a smile. "Got it. I'll bring the drinks to your table."

As I turn to go, Zerk sets down a white sack with what I assume is a take-out order. On his neck is a tattoo of a dragon with sharp teeth, long talons, and beady red eyes. The smell of French fries and a burger wafts out of the bag.

"Order's up for Baxter," he calls, looking at the table where my team is sitting. "Bax, are you here?"

I point to the beer garden. "I think he went out back with his buddies. We took his table."

I slide into my seat and lean back in the hard wooden chair. Every muscle aches. But our work is finished for today, and we can kick back. I blow out a breath and look around the table with a smile of pride.

I say, "Great work this week, guys. I appreciate all the effort you put into this project."

Bets brings over our drinks, and I raise a cold glass of pilsner.

I say, "You guys are the best. Thank you. Here's to you."

Mimi lifts a glass of Guinness. "Here, here."

Flora nods and toasts to the team.

Vincent sips his lager and sets it down. "It was dicey when the fire broke out. But it turned out fine."

Polly's negroni wobbles in her shaking hand. "I'm glad I survived the mob."

"Hell, yes," I say, "I'm glad we all survived."

We sip our drinks and nod, reflecting on the riots in town.

Mimi says to Polly, "If you do end up working with us, we'll teach you evasive maneuvers. But it sounds like they closed in on you fast, and you were trapped."

Polly nods and sits forward, sipping her cocktail.

We talk about the tension, troubles, and worries my mom and her friends brought to town. I cross my legs, and bob my foot. We're civilians at the moment and not on the clock. I'm starting to get a slight buzz from the beer when the front door of the bar opens.

A breeze blows in.

Five people in black clothes and face masks pulled over their heads step inside and stand by the door, checking out the pub.

A hush falls over the room as we all turn to look.

40

All I can see of the five newcomers' faces are their eyes and noses. In black jeans and t-shirts, they look fit. Their biceps are defined, and their thighs are strong, like you'd see on hard-riding mountain bicyclists.

I purse my lips. These are the anarchists. I've heard they're in their twenties and have an attitude.

A man in black saunters to a table near the door, where four gray-haired patrons look up with wide eyes. They set down their forks with a clatter.

A ketchup bottle skids to the floor.

The room is quiet. No one is talking now, or celebrating the end of the rioting.

The intruder looms over an older man. "Is this table taken?"

Chills sweep over me. I'd rather avoid conflict at the

moment. We're finding our groove and chilling out after a big job. Our energy is sapped. We've made it to the finish line, and we are done exerting ourselves.

I drum my fingers on the table and glance at my staff. Our gig might be wrapped up regarding the trade talks, but the town may need our services gratis.

We nod and hold eye contact with each other. Without speaking, we're in agreement and of one mind. The decision is made. If the situation escalates, we'll engage.

We set down our drinks and sit up straight, on alert. My muscles tense for a fight.

"Come on, grandad," the man dressed in black says. "You're almost done. Give it up for us."

He shakes the chair of the older gentleman, who rests a hand on his heart.

Bets marches over and snaps a bar rag in the air. "Knock it off. Don't bother the other customers. We're busy at the moment, so you'll have to wait to be seated, like everyone else does." She gestures to the bar, where three bar stools are vacant. "Sit there if you want while you wait."

"No," the guy says, "we wanted a table. We want this one, so we can look out the window."

Bets puts a hand on her hip. "I see, so you can watch for cops coming, and then run out and leave me stuck with the bill? Didn't your group do that yesterday? I'm not brilliant, but believe me, I can figure that out."

The anarchist shrugs. "I wasn't here. It must've been another group."

The air almost vibrates, the tension is so thick in the room.

I lean across the table and say in a low voice, "Let's move."

We stand and stride over, forming a line. We cross our arms and block the walkway to the back. Better to have them leave by the front door, the way they came in, than spread out and cause trouble in the bar.

Zerk comes out of the kitchen and says in a loud voice, "Sweetie pie, have you seen my gold nail clippers?" He stops in his tracks. His jaw drops.

Bets says, "We've got a situation here, and it seems to be a stand-off." She points. "That group wants this table, but these people aren't finished. What'd you think we should do?"

The anarchist whips off his face mask and shoves it in his back pocket. His face is whippet lean with a protruding nose. Rubbing his cleft chin, he looks to be in his late twenties.

"We didn't mean any harm, Pops," he says.

The four at the table stand.

The gray-haired man's hands shake. He says, "It's no problem. We were just leaving." One of the women has rosy cheeks. She frowns and clutches her purse under her arm, as if protecting it from thieves.

"Hey, hey," Zerk says, waving his hands and rushing over. "Let's settle down, shall we? We can all get along and drink together. No problem, right?"

Zerk points to the back door. "I've got a great spot for you guys. It's right outside, and you'll love it. Let's let these people finish their meal in peace. Come with me. Right this way. I'll tell you a funny story when we get out there. Just you wait, you'll love it."

Bets rolls her eyes and folds her arms.

The five people in black take off their masks and follow Zerk out back.

I massage my temples and marvel at their power trip meant to make a statement and intimate the rest of us. Hearty laughter floats in from the beer garden.

Bets grins at me. "You gotta love the guy. He can charm the pants off anyone." She hesitates and a flash of sadness crosses her face. "He would've made a great father."

I pat her arm. "He's the life of the party. You're lucky to have him."

"Most days," she says, wiping a tear from her eyes.

My team and I sit down at our table. People around us resume conversations. I take a slug of beer. Maybe it's possible for opposite sides to sit together in the same establishment and not get riled up. Zerk certainly is a peace-maker. City hall should have him run for mayor.

A woman sitting at the bar points at the television. She has long black hair and is wearing a brown plaid flannel shirt. She says, "They're showing something about Millersville. Can you turn up the volume?"

Bets grabs the remote and pushes buttons.

An anchor woman on TV gives us a bright white smile and says, "In breaking news after the riots in Millersville and protests that ripped through the town, we have a report the chief of police has just resigned. Let's go to the news conference happening right now."

Murmurs fly around the room. People talk in loud voices.

Bets says, "Keep it down. I want to hear what the police chief has to say for himself."

Like obedient grade school students, we close our mouths and listen.

The picture changes to a press conference being held outside our police station. The chief of police is worn and haggard, with dark circles under his eyes. He hunches over and runs a hand through his slick-back dark hair.

"I'm sad to announce that I've made the decision to step down after the events that took place in Millersville this week. The police response was not what it should have been, and the responsibility rests on my shoulders. Someone needs to take the blame, and I will do that. Effective immediately, I'm resigning from my post and turning the department over to my second-in-command."

The bar erupts with many voices talking at once. Someone cheers.

I clap a hand to my mouth and look at Mimi. "Can you

believe it? I didn't think he'd man up and take responsibility."

She says, "It's the right thing to do. He was responsible. He should've prepared better."

Vincent taps the table with a knuckle. "He should've called in the National Guard sooner and increased police presence on streets from the start. They were invisible when the anarchists roamed the streets. Where were the officers then?"

I sit back and stretch my arms in the air. "What a week this is turning out to be. By the way, Brinker says he wants to vote the mayor out of office in the next election."

Bets comes over and taps the back of my chair. "What do you guys think? Was that the right thing for him to do or not? While you were out there trying to save the day, I heard the mayor and police chief were golfing." She laughs. "They were going to stay out of town, and let the rest of us suffer."

She glances at the windows. "We're just lucky our windows are intact. Guess it pays to serve beer to both sides of the equation, the protesters and the enforcers, like you and your crew."

I whack the table with my hand. "I'm glad he stepped down. He could've and should've done better. I hope the next one in line learned a lesson, if the situation ever repeats itself."

Bets points at the TV. Everyone is talking loudly, and

we can't hear what the talking heads are saying. She says, "Isn't that your mother?"

I turn and gape. Yes, indeed. There's Daisy. She finally got her moment of five minutes of fame. "Yep, that's my mom." I grudgingly agree, "She does have a point. We could be kinder to the earth and not pollute as much. Drive less, walk more. Grow our own vegetables."

Mimi points a finger. "And don't use pesticides. Save the bees."

We hoist our drinks and drain them dry. "To saving the bees."

"Another round?" Bets says. "It's been a long week."

I glance around the table and have a sense it's time to disperse to our homes. Wrap it up, put a bow on it, and crash in bed for hours.

I say, "I think we'll skip it, but we'll be back another time for more. We're beat."

To my staff, I say, "Hey guys, why don't you take tomorrow off with pay? You deserve it."

We clap each other on the back, as mates who've been through an ordeal do, and walk out the door to return to the rest of our lives. The private and personal part of our lives can be in conflict with the demands of our work. We're driven to deliver results, but our families matter most.

Back home, I sink into a bubble bath and plan how to redecorate my home. A new shade of color on the taupe living room walls would be a nice change. And what will I do with my day off tomorrow? It'd be a shame to waste it by working and catching up on details.

I climb out of the bath and call my friend, Wendy, who owns a boat.

"How about going sailing tomorrow? Can you get time off?"

41

The next day just before noon, I leap out of bed and take a shower. A weight has been lifted off my shoulders, with the protests in the past, and I smile to myself as I slap together sandwiches. A day out on the water is just what I need.

My friend Wendy and I met when I first moved to town, and she lives on her boat. It's rare for her to take her boat out of the slip, so I appreciate her taking me for a day sail on short notice.

I drive west to Skyline Marina, park my car and hurry down the docks. When I jump on Wendy's boat, it rocks back and forth. The air is still, and I inhale the smell of briny sea air, my favorite scent. But there's no chance of sailing unless the wind picks up this afternoon.

"Hey you," she says, giving me a hug. "This is a wonderful surprise. If the wind kicks up, be prepared, because I'm in the mood to heel over and fly across the water."

"An excellent plan," I say with a grin. "I've been land bound for far too long. Especially this week." I open my arms and say, "Let me be free and ride with the wind."

She smacks my shoulder with a hand. "You don't have to be corny about it. Let's go. The engine's warmed up."

We cast off and make our way under power out of the marina.

"I packed lunch," I say. "Is hummus on pita bread okay with you? And black olives on the side?"

She shrugs. "Sure, that's what I always order at the Brown Lantern."

"Speaking of that," I say. "You won't believe what happened there last night."

When I tell her about the anarchists and how Bets and Zerk reacted, she says, "My aunt and uncle were there. They said it was weird, how the guy wanted their table. But I guess it worked out. Weirdos, you know?"

Thinking about the Brown Lantern makes me think of my half-sister Karina who runs Gigi's Cafe. She has no idea, as far as I can tell, that we're related. I would hate to demolish her cherished memories of childhood. Talk about breaking the piggy bank wide open with a hammer.

I take a slow breath and say, "If you were related to someone, but they didn't know it, how would you approach it?"

She slows our speed. "Are you talking about Karina,

who runs Gigi's Café?"

My mouth falls open. "Wait, how did you know?"

She waves a hand. "Just an educated guess. Anyone who looks at you two carefully would notice. You look alike. You have the same nose."

A chill runs up my spine, and I clamp my mouth shut.

She says, "Just go talk with her. Take her out for coffee. Or go to the Brown for a beer. Be straight with her. Don't pussy foot around the facts."

I glance toward the cabin leading to her quarters below and change the subject. "How's your cat?"

"He hates sailing, but he's okay under power. Don't worry about him. He's probably in my bed, nestled under the blankets. But let's talk about you, what are you going to do about Karina?"

My stomach churns. My gut aches. My eye twitches. I don't want to take this brave step forward.

I stare at a forested island and say, "I'll have to think about how to approach her."

"Don't think, just do," she says. "The wind's coming up, so let's sail down Rosario Strait."

We race across the water for a few hours, grinning and letting out the sails, hauling in the lines. After our sail, my body is light. I can breathe easier. It feels like I just had a vacation.

I step on the dock, and thank her and head home. My body feels like it's one with the Salish Sea. The knots in my neck are gone.

Driving down Commercial, I mull over my life. Maybe I'll join the Chamber of Commerce and network, like Brinker suggested. It wouldn't be so bad to get to know other business owners in the area. I could use a support system of fellow minded souls.

Painting crews are working on buildings downtown. Graffiti and slogans spray painted on walls disappear under fresh coats of paint.

Back at home, I open a can of paint and roll color over the mess on the walls left by Daisy's friends. I'm using an aquamarine color to liven up the place. It's already making me smile as I cover the walls.

The doorbell rings. I'm not expecting anyone, but I set the roller down in the metal pan and look out the window. A florist's truck is out front.

Opening the door, I greet a man wearing a cowboy hat, which is unusual in these parts.

"Violet Cleveland?" he says with a dimpled smile.

"That's me."

"Delivery for you." He hands me a vase with blue daisies, baby's breath, and a single white rose.

"Thanks," I say.

"Enjoy."

He returns to his white van, whistling all the way.

I take the flowers inside and shut the door. Opening a card, I read a note: "Sorry I broke into your house. I hope you'll find it in your heart to forgive me. Love, Daisy"

I toss the card on my desk and cross my arms. I'm not

ready to forgive her, but I still love her. She's the one who raised me and stuck with me after my father left.

She was wrong to trash my place, but I won't freeze her out. I'll stay in touch because she's family. She's who she is, and no matter what I say, she's not likely to change.

Speaking of family reminds me of Karina at Gigi's Café. I'm nervous about telling my half-sister that our stories are linked. But I hope I'll grow into initiating a discussion about that in time.

I smile as an idea comes to me.

I pick up my phone and text a number.

"Thanks for the flowers."

Thanks for reading this! Please let other readers know what to expect by posting reviews on Goodreads, Amazon and Bookbub.

Read Secrets at the Cafe to find out what happens next!

If you enjoyed The Mother's Threat, sign up for my author newsletter on my website www.susanspechtoram.com to be the first to hear about my other books.

Follow me on BookBub for more updates!

ABOUT THE AUTHOR

Susan is writing mysteries, thrillers, and suspense novels. Previously, she served as senior director of corporate communications for biotechnology companies. Susan worked as an activity aide in an upscale nursing home's psychiatric unit. She was a potter and painter with an art studio in Seattle and has also been a market researcher, a nurse's aide, and a waitress. Her essays have been published in Mothering Magazine, Twins Magazine and Utne Reader.

Susan grew up near Detroit, Michigan and received a BFA with Honors from University of Oregon and a MBA in Marketing from Seattle University. She lives in a windy part of the Pacific Northwest with her husband and their rescue dog.

BOOKS BY SUSAN SPECHT ORAM

Shore Lodge, a high-stakes psychological thriller

The Thieves, a high-stakes entertaining heist thriller

Cabin Eight, a speculative psychological thriller

The Mother's Threat, a compelling domestic thriller

Secrets at the Cafe, a novel of suspense about family and friendship

Under Jackson Bridge, a thriller

Humorous fiction:

Boating with Buddy, a report from a canine correspondent

Nonfiction:

Brief business books on investor relations, crisis communication and public relations

9 798987 041079